Suicide of the Month

Suicide of the Month

R. T. Barnes

Contents

Friendship Now!

O N THE CONGENIALITY scale, I'd give myself a solid eight out of ten. I know I've got my faults, that I'm not always as nice or helpful as I could be. Looking back on some situation or other, I know there are times when I could have done better. Like when that disabled person with the strange legs was waiting to cross the road and I didn't stop—I just forced a weak smile and unenthusiastic wave as I drove past. I could barely sleep that night. I try to be better than that, and more often than not, I succeed. I do my best.

Now, some people just aren't very nice at all. They don't even make any effort to get along with the rest of us. They feel no shame. Just flat-out mean people. I've never understood what motivates them. Take the woman at the Shop Mart, for instance. She gives me the nastiest look every time I go in there. She has a mean little face to begin with, but she dresses it up with heaping globs of scorn and ill will. She's not like that with everyone; with other customers, she merely radiates a low-intensity ennui, but she has a special bucket of bile for me. I don't know what to think about it anymore. She barely even looks at me. I try my best to be friendly; I always give her a cheerful "Good morning to you!" and I say "please" and "thank you" with the same élan that I shower all my other human brothers and sisters with. She just mumbles and turns her puffy red face away, as if she hadn't heard. Why, once she just about tore off my finger taking a five-dollar bill from my hand. I was buying the morning paper, as anyone is entitled to do, but she made me feel as if I were some kind of awful monster—a rapist or murderer. Sorry, I was just trying to buy the paper, ma'am.

One morning last weekend, as I was having my first cigarette of the day on the back deck, my neighbor Derek came out with a large bong and motioned with his head that I was quite welcome to join him. He even made a motion to pass the bong across decks. I politely declined, and he then explained that he only smoked on the weekend, as a reward for his hard work all week. I knew this to be false, I had often seen him on his deck with the bong during the week, even before work sometimes, with him never failing to offer to share with me even though I always decline the offer, but I kept this to myself. We smiled at each other—all in all a pleasant exchange. His face never gets all red and puffy.

The woman at the Shop Mart hasn't always hated me. She used to be nice. Well, she was *okay*, at least. She used to look me in the eye, even smile now and again—once she even asked how my day was. It's the kind of thing that makes one feel safe and secure in their own little nook of society.

I must admit, if I am to be truly honest with myself, I may know what caused all these problems in the first place. One morning I was in a bit of a hurry and didn't have time to wait for the dark roast vanilla coffeepot to completely fill up, the machine was still dripping into the pot, you understand, not much but enough to cause that sizzle you get when the new coffee drips hit the heating pad. I knew it was the wrong thing to do, but dammit, I was in a hurry, and what's a little bit of sizzling? Well, quite a bit it turns out. My little lady of the Shop Mart went into a tizzy and laid it all out for me. You see, it turns out that once you put the coffeepot back on the heating pad, those little sizzling drips of coffee burn themselves right to the bottom of the pot, and if you're having a bad day, then when someone removes that pot again, the whole bottom can come off, spilling hot coffee everywhere and creating a big mess, a mess that someone is going to have to clean up. And guess who gets the job?

I didn't know about that, and I told her so, with full apologies. She hasn't looked me in the eyes since. She probably wishes I were dead.

I've never had anyone harbor such an ill will toward me, and so I decided to do something about it. I started with a little research, to find out more about this strange, angry person. The first thing was to find out her name. Of course, it's right there on her name tag, but somehow I'd never bothered to look. I was shocked at my own indifference and decided that I'd deserved at least a week's worth of shunning just for that. I am nothing if not fair.

It turned out that her name was Mahal, and after a quick Google at home, it was revealed that Mahal is a Filipino name, meaning I love you. It seems inappropriate and really misguided. A more apt name would have been Amihan, Tagalog for "northeast monsoon."

I wondered if anger and vitriol were common traits of all Filipinos, the way that discipline and an unwavering obedience to strong military-minded leaders is a common trait of Germans. I researched the Philippines further; the twelfth most populous country in the world with a population of ninety million, a gross national product of $327.2 billion, former colony of both Spain and the United States, but shaped most by Spain's three-hundred-year reign. That was all very well, but it didn't tell me much about why Mahal hates me so much. I posted on ESL message boards questions like, "Are Filipinos generally angry and abusive?" To which I received only a few replies, all of which from white supremacist groups that didn't mention Filipinos specifically but included them in a larger group of non-Caucasian peoples to which they were staunchly opposed. Hardly a nonbiased sample group, in any case.

It was clear—if I was going to learn more about the people of the Philippines, then I was going to have to roll up my sleeves, pull up my socks, and wade into the masses. So I bought a do-it-yourself Web site creator CD and founded the From the Philippines to the World Friendship Society. Within days I was inundated with requests for membership, many of which were from native Filipinos, often with marriage proposals. Within a week I was forced to exclude all non-Canadian resident applicants. We had a very lively forum, and it turned out that Filipinos are not generally angry. This was quite a blow for me. I had hoped that Mahal hated me out of a trait inherent to her people. No, I made many new and cheerful friends on the FTPTTWFS, and so it meant that there was something about *me*, personally, that made Mahal's face so red and puffy. However, I couldn't be completely sure; perhaps there was something I was still missing.

I organized dinner parties and strategy sessions for the FTPTTWFS, all with the goal of finding ways to bridge the gap not only between the Philippines and myself, but between the Philippines and the world itself. Sadly, within several months the group dwindled to only four members: myself, Ryan Sevilla, Jesus Navarro, and Jeremy Taylor, the last of the Caucasian holdouts, desperately clinging to the hope that he might yet find a young Filipino wife.

The whole thing was beginning to seem pointless. I had learned that Filipino people were not generally mean, and that Mahal was simply an unhappy person who did not like me because I prematurely poured a cup of coffee. But perhaps there was still something more that I could gain. Since I'd already put the work in, I could use the FTPTTWFS to forge a bond with Mahal, to reach out to her personally, first as a Caucasian Canadian to a Filipino immigrant, and then as one human being to another, I could shine a spotlight of amity upon her scarred soul.

I organized a "Friendship Run" for the remaining members of the FTPTTWFS. Not a marathon by any means, just a few city blocks, but designed to end precisely in front of the main window of the Shop Mart.

I had arranged for the local beat reporter from the free weekly paper *The Community Times* to meet us for a quick interview, as well as one reporter from the local multicultural television channel.

I felt like a world changer for the several minutes it took the FTPTTWFS and me to run our course. I'd had T-shirts made for all four of us, but only three of us showed up for the event; Jeremy had called earlier to inform me that he was quitting the group as he would be focusing solely on the Web site Korean Friend Finder. Even if there'd been four of us, it still wouldn't have warranted a police escort, the way a traditional parade would, so we kept to the side of the road, trying not to impede the traffic as we trotted along with our Friendship Now! placards.

At the Shop Mart I introduced myself to the confused beat reporter, who kept looking over my shoulder as if he'd expected something more. "Yes, sir, this is all of us," I declared, holding my temper, which I forgive myself for, considering the stress I was under. And then I noticed that Ryan and Jesus had disappeared, with their official FTPTTWFS T-shirts, for which I had not yet been reimbursed. Their placards lay in a muddy puddle in the gutter. From the corner of my eye I spotted the TV news van pull up across the street. The reporter and cameraman approached me and then suddenly seemed to change their minds. They turned and quickly got back into the van and drove off. The beat reporter had silently sneaked away into the store and was reading a magazine about tattoos. Nobody cared.

I swooped down and rescued the placards from the filthy street, held them high and, in a powerful and urgent roar, demanded, "FRIENDSHIP NOW! FRIENDSHIP NOW! FRIENDSHIP NOW!" Finally I had the world's attention. I marched into the shop and declared, "FRIENDSHIP NOW! WHERE IS MAHAL?"

There was no one behind the counter, but the door to the back room was ajar, and a pair of frightened Filipino eyes stared back at me. She asked in a quavering voice, "Who are you?"

"Tell me the truth, Mahal, yes, I know your name, it's right there on your name tag, tell me the truth. Do you hate me?"

Her answer came back to me strong and blunt; her word was a frying pan striking my forehead.

"Yes!"

"I'm sorry about the coffee drips! Forgive me! I knew not what I did!"

The door closed, and I heard the lock turn.

What could I do but leave? I left like a mouse, feeling eyes boring into me, judging me, rating me. I felt like a real zero on the congeniality scale. I didn't even want to think about what had happened, about how all of my best intentions had gone awry. I slunk home, placards left in the Dumpster behind the Shop Mart.

I wanted to be alone in my apartment, to put on the TV and fade away into some reality show purgatory; but before I could put my key in the door, my neighbor Derek came scuttling down the hall, with Pam and Joseph, my neighbors on the other side, looking nervous and desultory, their heads down, in tow. Derek grabbed my arm and said, "I need you to come inside for a minute. They're coming in too."

I didn't ask why; there was an urgency to him that I didn't dare question. Once inside, I stood near the door with Pam and Joseph as Derek stood across the room from us. He said, "I'm a drug addict."

We, Derek's confessors, stood silent for an awkward moment and then Pam applauded him, clapping enthusiastically. "That's very brave, Derek, I think this is an excellent step," she said.

I quickly seconded her motion and clapped a few times for good measure. I must confess, I'd had no idea that marijuana was addictive, or addictive enough for someone to proclaim himself an actual *addict*. I considered asking if he were smoking crack or heroin on the side but killed the thought. It was not my place. It was enough that this brave man was reaching out for help, reaching out a hand to those he had chosen, those who he instinctually understood would be there for him. It was a bit strange given that I certainly didn't know anything about him other than that he seemed to love smoking pot. But here he was looking for empathy and solidarity, which every human being craves, and I felt the warmth of human kinship in my heart.

"If you see me out on that deck with a bong, I'd like you to call the police. Could you do that for me?"

Pam and Joseph hemmed and hawed at the request, but I readily agreed, and then walked over and gave him a hug and many encouraging pats on the back. "Friendship Now!" I cried. "Friendship Now!"

Lawn

I SPEND A LOT of time working on my yard. I like a nice green lawn. And just the right length too. If it's too long then people might think you're a couple of days late mowing, and that's the last thing I need. Too short and it ruins the lushness that I have worked so hard to attain. I don't mean to blow my own horn, but I actually modified the chassis on my mower to get my own custom length. None of the presettings satisfied me. That's just the way I am, call me a perfectionist. A great lawn doesn't just happen to a man, you can't leave it to nature; it must be shaped and molded with an iron will, the kind of will that pushes a great baseball player or a top corporate executive. It says a lot about a man the kind of lawn he keeps. Like my neighbor, you can tell from one look at the chaos he calls a backyard that he doesn't have his shit together. He doesn't care about his lawn or anything else. It's all written there in the undisciplined tangle of anarchy that he calls a backyard. What's he doing with his time? Probably carousing, not taking things seriously. I barely even see him around here anymore, he's always off somewhere, having a good old time. My father always taught me, "Son, there's one thing you must remember in life, and if you do as I say, you'll always know that you're on the right track. Lawn first, everything else second. It's the mark of a man."

Late last night I climbed over his fence with my push mower. It was a beautiful clear night with a full moon, I must say that I felt more alive than I had in a while. It was time I took things into my own hands. I'm not the type to sit by idly and watch the world go to hell. But sweet Jesus, from the way my neighbor acts, you wouldn't even know that something was wrong! Last month I saw him out front and just in passing I mentioned his lawn could use a little attention. Bastard just grinned and nodded like some kind of moron, got into his freaking Volvo, and drove off like he didn't have a care in the world. Am I wrong to take this as a personal insult? This is my cul-de-sac too. In fact, it's far more my cul-de-sac. Who organized the communal lawn sale? It took a lot of prodding and shaming to get everyone to work together for that common goal. But not so much as an old pair of suspenders on my good neighbor's lawn. Probably out rock climbing with a teenage girl that he met in some hip bar, but the joke's on him because as it turns out she's a lesbian, and she thought he was a homosexual because of those expensive jeans that he wears. That wouldn't surprise me the least bit.

And not everyone has it so fortunate. Why, just this morning while I was getting my cup of joe, I saw this poor soul with no arms. He was reading a newspaper with his feet! Can you believe that? No arms and reading a paper, turning the pages with his feet. Now that's real courage. I don't know if he has a lawn, or if he's able to mow it, but I wouldn't bet against him. He has something my neighbor knows nothing about—pride. I was so impressed that I told him right then and there that I'd be honored if he came over and mowed my lawn, just because I've always admired a man who knows how to handle a big old gas mower. I suppose I must not have explained myself very well, but let's not talk about that now. Well, let's just say we weren't on the same page, which is a shame considering that he is a veteran—that is at least my assumption.

Can you imagine a brave man like that, reading a newspaper with his feet, and there my neighbor is not even mowing his lawn! That's why I had to mow it myself last night. There were no lights on in his house, so

I supposed that he must have been out with one of his hipster friends. I'd been up alone in the den, watching old family videos; and then when I went into the kitchen, I caught a glimpse of that yard in the glorious light of the moon—it was beautiful and tragic all at once, like that picture of that naked child running down the road during the Vietnam War. I stood awed and confused for a moment, and then I acted, and in that moment I knew that I was born for such perfect bubbles of time. I crept out into my yard. I wasn't wearing shoes; I knew that socks would be quieter. Silently easing the small push mower (it has been in the family for five generations), I slipped over the fence and began to mow. It felt good out there in the moonlight and cool, crisp air. It felt ancient and timeless, almost godlike. Suddenly, instinctively, I shed my robe and stood there naked and powerful, a man in charge of his destiny.

Parallax Shift

J OHN TRIED NOT to think about things like threesomes with girls at the office or killing his nemesis, Charles in accounting, in a drunken bar fight for which he could not be held accountable, as he was only defending himself from a man clearly filled with hate and rage. A mean and petty man.

John was successful in business and also a reliable family man. He had never really wanted either of those things—not in the sense of something that you crave or dream about—just in the sense that they're things that one should aspire toward. He had never followed his instincts because they had always seemed irrational, like groping his niece's perfect pear-shaped ass or taking the kid's college fund down to Vegas for a big score.

One Saturday morning, his paper did not arrive. He felt a deep rage toward the paperboy, but he hid it from his family. He would have been mildly ashamed had he known that the paperboy was dead. He'd died the night before in his sleep, along with the rest of his family, as the result of a broken gas pipe. John would never know this story, even though it would later be featured prominently in the local newspaper.

That morning at the local convenience store, he bought a Scratch and Win lottery ticket. He had never bought such a thing because he knew that gambling was irrational, and that he shouldn't waste his hard-earned money. For a reason that he could not identify, perhaps a long suppressed impulse, he bought a ticket along with his morning paper. He scratched it right there at the counter and found that he had won $500. John was then happy that the paper hadn't arrived that morning.

After breakfast that morning, John walked away from it all. He followed a sudden instinct and left his wife and children at the breakfast table and walked into the street without saying a word. He was relieved that they didn't follow him. He walked and walked, just as his instincts told him to. He walked all the way downtown and then booked himself into a midrange hotel. There was no reason for choosing that particular hotel other than that it simply felt like the right place to be. In the room's trash can by the desk, he noticed a book of crosswords, and he picked it out and inspected it. It was a large book with hundreds of puzzles, but only one clue attempted—a three letter answer for the clue "large bird" that was inexplicably filled in as "cat." Perhaps this was some sort of joke or the work of a young child, he wondered to himself. John roughly wrote the word "emu" over the top and was pleased to find that it worked out with the surrounding answers. That night, before falling into a peaceful slumber, he completed the puzzle.

The next morning he continued on his walk. He walked through downtown and then across a bridge and into suburbs again. He walked until dark and then felt a strong urge to go up the driveway of the house he was passing. He felt that he should try the door and did. It was unlocked—in the living room he found an old man hanging by a rope from the light fixture. The man was quite dead and clearly had been for some days, judging from the odor. A window was open, and the body swayed slightly in the draft. In the middle of the room was a large trunk with a note on top. John read, "I hereby confess to the sin of slowly poisoning my wife with household cleaning products. She deserved a much better and more patient husband than me, lo all these many decades. Although, I must admit that I found her to be a most unpleasant companion. In this trunk lies the ill-gotten spoils of my plot. I assume it will be returned to the insurance company. I resign!"

R. T. BARNES

John didn't think much about what he did next. He cut down the body of the old man and dragged it to the basement where he wasn't at all surprised to discoverer a freezer. He barely managed to fit the body into it, although he had to rearrange various bags of frozen vegetables, such as corn and cauliflower. Fortunately, the old man was quite small. Next, he ordered a pizza and then spent the rest of the evening lounging on the couch while he ate and slowly solved another crossword. He slept well that night.

For several months John lived in the old man's house. It was a relief to not have to work anymore or talk to anyone—nobody even knew where he was. He didn't worry about friends or family of the old man visiting or about being arrested; his instincts told him he was perfectly secure.

Every night John solved one crossword. The crosswords were not very difficult, he knew that. John was a humble man and knew that there were others who were very much better than him at solving puzzles, and this did not bother him at all. He often said to himself, "I bet that if I were to enter into a crossword competition, then I'd probably be one of the worst. I wouldn't win anything at all, and I don't give a damn. It's not about that." When he wasn't sleeping or solving puzzles, he looked through photo albums and made the appropriate exclamations for each picture, such as, "Look how young and handsome you were," and "Your wife was quite a peach!" Or something like "Oh, I've always wanted to travel to Paris, you're so lucky!" John liked to rummage around through all the old man's things. John was content to live in a dead man's house and felt that it was just where he was supposed to be.

One day his instinct gripped him again, and he simply walked out in the middle of dinner, Chinese food, paid for with insurance cash. He left with nothing but the old man's clothes that he was wearing and a book of crosswords tucked into his back pocket. John followed his instincts for a long time and walked through many neighborhoods and then out of the city and into the woods. He walked through the woods for many days, surviving on berries that he assumed were not poisonous and drinking from streams that he assumed were not polluted. One day he came upon a compound and knew that he had found his new home. There were no roads connected to the little circular gathering of cabins. The words New Jerusalem were painted on a piece of plywood nailed to a tree. John then understood that this was a religious compound. He whispered to himself, "A Christian cult," and nodded with satisfaction at his powers of deduction. In the center of the compound, there were six long tables and scattered about the long grass were many bones. John inspected the remains and recognized them as human. He observed, "Clearly a person's skull," or "This looks like a leg bone," or "These hand bones are completely intact." Thoughts of mass ritual suicide occupied John's thoughts as he looked through the cabins before settling on the largest as his new abode. His cabin had fallen into some disrepair, and he immediately began to clean out the insects and a dead bat with a straw broom. John slept very well that night.

There were many dusty old Bibles lying about, but John had not the slightest desire to read them. He did however find a diary—that of the cult's leader, a man named Jeremiah Smith, and John read a little of that every night before finishing his crossword. Jeremiah had once been a businessman, just like John. Jeremiah had also felt a sudden calling and left everything behind, but unlike John, he had taken his family with him, as well as several other families from his church. Jeremiah had convinced them, along with his family, that he was a prophet and that they should do as he said, even if it meant moving out into the wilderness. He had also convinced them that they should all poison themselves along with himself. He felt this was an excellent opportunity for getting into heaven. After reading the diary, John had no doubts about Jeremiah's

R. T. BARNES

sincerity, and he certainly wished he and his followers nothing but the best.

Fortunately for John, the cult members had left a large supply of canned and dehydrated food. There was a well with a hand pump for freshwater, and so he lived in relative comfort. Once again he had arrived at a place that seemed to be exactly where he should be, and John was more than satisfied.

He lived there through the fall, and then when the snow fell, he went out each day to collect firewood to burn in the iron stove of his cabin. At night he would bundle himself up with many blankets borrowed from all of the dead former inhabitants of New Jerusalem. His supply of canned and dried foods kept him well fed and healthy, but on some nights he dreamed of bologna sandwiches on thick slices of freshly baked white bread with lots of mayonnaise or Caesar salads topped with hots chunks of Cajun chicken. But John never wanted to leave because he had that comfortable, pleasant, secure feeling that came with following his instinct.

When spring came and the snows had melted away, he knew that it was time to move on once again. He woke up one morning and simply headed off into the wilderness in the direction that seemed right. He smiled pleasantly and hummed "Reflex" by Duran Duran as he walked. After two days, he came to a highway and felt that he should put his thumb out whenever a car passed by. Eventually one car stopped for him, and when the driver asked where John was headed to, he replied, "Just following my instincts. I'll tell you when I need to get out." The driver was then frightened of John, and they didn't speak at all after that. It hadn't been a normal answer—it was not *right*. It was enough to make suspicion percolate through his brain. The driver thought that John might do some of the things he had seen hitchhikers do in horror movies. He imagined that John must have some sort of exotic knife that he performed his atrocities with. At the next town that they came to, John knew it was time to get out of the car, and the driver was relieved. He would tell the story of how he had survived the experience to his wife. That night he Googled the official FBI Web site for the Ten Most Wanted List. He went to bed disappointed that he had not found John's picture there.

John had been dropped off across from a large building that looked to him like a warehouse. He walked up to the door, and finding it unlocked, he let himself in. It was a large and almost empty warehouse. In the middle of the space was a wall of computers, a desk with computers, and a slouched figure sat before it. A large metal cylinder sat nose up on a stage, tapered at the top; John immediately recognized it as a rocket. Upon closer inspection, the slouched figure was a scientist. John knew this because the corpse was dressed in a white lab coat, which he knew was the preferred mode of dress for scientists. The body did not smell at all and looked newly dead. John turned his attention to the spaceship. He walked up the stairs and onto the stage and noticed a red button on the rocket ship's shiny silver side; he pushed it, and a door swung open with a clang and a rush of air. *Obviously*, John thought to himself, *I should step inside.* There was not much room, just enough for a comfortable leather recliner and a small dashboard of various instruments. John sat in the chair, buckled himself in, and pressed a green button prominently featured on the panel. The door clanged shut, a great roar of engines and ignition suddenly sounded, and John felt himself being pushed down in the seat by the g-forces of liftoff. He knew that he was going into space. He was not shocked by it the least; it was where he was supposed to go.

Sadly, there were no windows to view the stars by, and so he pulled his book of crosswords from his pocket and began to solve a new puzzle. Eventually he noticed the effects of g-force again and knew that he would soon land. He braced himself just before the rocket came to a violent stop, hitting solid earth, falling onto its side and rolling, buttons and dials falling off the console, and dents pushed into the rocket walls. When it stopped rolling, the door sprang open with a rush of air.

John had some difficulty extricating himself from the various safety belts and harnesses as he was hanging upside down but managed the last of the latches and fell with a thump, banging his forehead. A moderately sized egg formed and, while exploring it with his fingers noted, "Well, it's about time I had one of these." He scrambled out of the rocket and found himself in the middle of an alien city. Pastel-colored skyscrapers with round windows rose to impossible heights all around him. Clear tubes snaked through the city, appearing to float in midair. Upon the shiny metal streets were thousands of idling buggies gently humming and hovering just above the ground. John thought they looked like the bumper cars that he'd ridden at various fairs in his youth. With a tinge of excitement, he climbed aboard one. He wasn't surprised that the controls were just like an Earth bumper car. He drove up the street, carefully navigating the idle cars.

He stopped at the entrance to a building and, leaving the car behind, stepped in. There was no lobby, just an intricate network of corridors flanked with small rooms, none of which had a door, just circular openings. In each room there was a small round table in the middle with several mummified bodies. They were obviously alien corpses, what with the unusually large and bulbous head, three eye stalks, and four arms apiece. "The air is very hot and dry, perfect for the mummification process," John noted to himself. Everywhere he went, he found the same thing. It was clear that the whole city was dead, probably another mass suicide—but on a much larger scale. Satisfied with his inspection, he went back out into the street and turned his attention to one of the hovering tubes. Reaching the opening, he was immediately sucked in and hurtled along, first through the city, and then out and across a wide barren landscape of purple dunes, and then vast fields of cracked blue earth. Then another city, just like the first, rapidly grew in the distance, and soon he was spat out onto another city street. He'd found the experience exhilarating and soothing at once, and only regretted that he'd banged his head again as he hit the ground. He had a mild headache.

John walked into the nearest building and understood that it was a kind of theater. There was a large screen with images of various geometric shapes, all pastel colored, that spun and sidled across the screen and exchanged forms. It was silent; he wondered if the aliens had ears. There was no seating. This was a mystery, but he wasn't too bothered by it. John stood and watched the shapes for a while, finding that they soothed his headache. A slight movement near the opposite wall drew his attention. A figure stood still watching the screen. It had a bulbous head, three eye stalks, and four arms. John walked up smiling and introduced himself, extending his hand. "I'm John," he proudly announced. The alien seemed to ignore him. John cleared his throat and repeated. Again nothing, the alien stood stock-still and stared at the screen with all three eyes. "Can you hear sounds?" John asked. Nothing. When he stood in front of the alien, blocking its view, it immediately turned and waddled out of the theater. John followed close behind. The moment he left the theater, his headache reasserted itself. The alien jumped into a buggy and rode away, John still in pursuit. It entered the tallest structure on the street, and John followed it into what looked like an elevator, which it was. He stood beside the being as they rose, repeatedly introducing himself, extending his hand and tapping it on something like a shoulder, all to no avail. His head was now throbbing powerfully; he felt nauseous and a little dizzy. He realized it was the first time since he'd begun his journey that he'd suffered any real discomfort at all. The elevator stopped at the roof, and he followed the alien as it waddled straight to the edge and hopped off. He peered over

R. T. BARNES

and watched as it splattered on the steel street below. John was puzzled, and he sat down to ponder it, but he could think of nothing past the awful throbbing of his brain. Blood dripped from his nose. He took the book of crosswords from his back pocket but couldn't focus on the page. All was a blur of pastels. It seemed urgent to him to finish the last crossword clue, the only one left in the book, but he could not focus. He wept. It occurred to him that he hadn't thought about threesomes or killing Charles for a long time. He remembered the moment when the whole chain of events had started—the morning that his paper had not arrived. It occurred to him that maybe the paperboy had died. He held the crossword in front of his face but still could not focus or even remember what the final clue had been. John stood up and walked over the edge. It felt like the right thing to do.

Suicide of the Month

ANOTHER THREE PEOPLE killed themselves at the office today. As for me, I'm sitting back and taking it easy with a cold one. I've got twenty bucks on the game tonight, and I picked up a five pound microwave lasagna for dinner. The whole night is set out, all the things I like to do, all the things that relax me. I barely feel like killing myself at all. Of course, it is there in the back of my mind, as it always is for everyone. But the dark voice is quiet tonight and is merely whispering to me, *Do it, do it, do it, do it*, sweetly and gently. Yesterday it was positively screaming! "END IT ALL NOW DO IT DO IT PUT A KNIFE POINT UP ON THE TABLE AND SMASH YOUR EYE DOWN ONTO IT!" That was quite a day yesterday, a lot of back orders.

Incidentally, that knife thing was how John killed himself today. It's odd because I didn't mention anything yesterday about having an overarching impulse to do it myself. We both thought of exactly the same thing within a day of each other. Strange coincidence.

Maryanne blew her head off with a shotgun in the lunch room—pretty standard stuff. Left a note about not being able to take the pain and loneliness any longer, yada-yada, etc. Her husband killed himself last year and left a note about how he couldn't stand living with her anymore and that he'd wasted his life. Turned out he'd wanted to be a jazz musician, but that all went south once Maryanne had gotten pregnant. Funny thing is, Maryanne always said she was going to kill herself because of her husband, and once he died she seemed to cheer up quite a bit, and so we all figured she'd have at least another five years before she blew her head off. So it was slightly unexpected, although she had always proclaimed the shotgun to be her preferred method of suicide.

Young Brandon from the mail room electrocuted himself in the basement. Only twenty-two years old and burned to a crisp in the basement. He'd barely had time to suffer, and he just went ahead and lit himself up like a lightbulb—I think we all admire him for that. A good kid. There was still that cooked Brandon smell down there at the end of the day. I'm going to put a letter in recommending him for Suicide of the Month, I think he's earned it.

The hockey game is just about to start, and I'm really looking forward to the distraction it will bring. Last game was a real doozy. It was tied 2-1 in the third period when our captain, Markus Naslund, scored with only three seconds left to send it to overtime; and then on the ensuing face-off, he completely ignored the puck, took off his skate, and slashed his own throat right there at center ice! Then our mascot, Fin, went down and rolled all over in the blood, which must have been great for the kids. The crowd went wild. I wish I'd been there to see it live.

I watched a great documentary last night. I love sports, but I also like to learn, and so I watch a lot of documentaries. That one was about a bonobo monkey called Alex that they taught sign language. When they first took him out of the wild, he was just an ordinary monkey. He didn't know anything. Then they taught him to read and to communicate through sign language. He told them all about himself. He said that when he was in the wild he was quite happy, that he just liked to eat and sleep and have sex with other monkeys; but once he was captured and taught to read and communicate with sign words, he started hearing little voices in his head that told him to hang himself from the top of the cell with a piece of string that the researchers had given him to play with. He said it was mostly because of all the intelligence tests they made him do. So eventually they came up with a game where Alex had to solve a logic problem and then they would give him a sleeping pill. Every time he solved a problem, they'd give him another sleeping pill and he'd save it up. Soon he had a big bowl of pills and was able to overdose. The experiment was a big success and apparently a real breakthrough in the study of human evolution. The desire to kill oneself goes back millions of years to our common ancestor with chimps.

No intellectual pursuits tonight though, just hockey and a cold brew. I'm really just killing time until the weekend when I'm having my suicide party. I finally got a whole weekend off, so on Friday it's preparation for the party, suicide Saturday night, and then the funeral on Sunday. I think it's going to be great. Everyone from the office has promised to come and all my friends too. Well, actually the only friends I have are people from the office, but hey, it's the same with everyone else in the world, right? I know it's selfish of me, but I wish Jerry from accounting had waited a couple of weeks before injecting himself with that massive overdose of speed and heroin. He was a real party animal and funny as hell. My brother and the two other surviving members of my family (second cousins) have promised to make it down.

Thompson, over on the second floor, is a part-time carpenter; and I paid him a hundred bucks to make me a big wooden cross for my crucifixion on Saturday night. I know that some people think crucifixion is a little gaudy, you know, like showing off, but I've always liked the ritual of it—I'm a Catholic through and through. Tradition is important to me. I like to do things right, and this feels right. So after the limbo contest—hopefully everyone will be good and tipsy by then and ready to really party—I'm going straight up onto that cross where I can watch all the drunken craziness, tap my head to the music, and slowly slip away into oblivion. Hopefully I'll be dead by morning, but just in case, my brother is bringing an industrial nail gun to finish me off.

Well, it looks like the game is starting, so I'd better get the lasagna into the oven and grab myself another beer. Go, Canucks, go!

The Hidden Function

I WON'T LIE TO you. I wanted to spy on my neighbors. There was a big fifteen-story apartment building across the street from my old place. It was absolutely full of weirdos and perverts. Behind all of those dozens of windows things were happening—dirty little secrets and the like. Things had to be happening. Interesting, bad things.

I've learned in my life that people are bad, sometimes wicked. Just take a look at the newspapers—theft, rape, murder. And let's not forget about satanic cults. Statisticians say that 40 percent of married couples have at least one member who has been unfaithful, so it's just a mathematical fact that when you have a large group of people behind a large number of windows, then there has to be at least a few people having intercourse with the wrong people. I knew that it had to be so. And I wanted to watch them. This is my weakness, my sin, and I have to live my life knowing that in some small way I am just as flawed and wicked as the masses.

Of course, people usually close their blinds and curtains when they are doing bad things, but not always, and often there is a small crack through which one can see. I will admit that I cannot look at a window with curtains *almost* closed without feeling a strong sexual charge. It's like the slit up the side of a skirt revealing the tantalizing promise of more and more thigh, like the hint of cleavage—it's the promise of strange lands and customs, something that you didn't know before.

I bought a fine pair of high-powered binoculars, the best available in my price range. I can see very well with them. I should say that I *could* see very well with them, back in those days. I don't have binoculars anymore.

To start with, I designated each window a letter and number, as on a spreadsheet. A-G on the x-axis and 1-15 on the Y. This system would greatly facilitate good record keeping of the events witnessed. On my first night of surveillance, I prepared a large thermos of coffee, several tuna sandwiches with celery and mustard individually wrapped in wax paper, and a bucket for urination. Earlier in the day, while walking home from the office, I'd spotted the bucket at a construction site just a few blocks from home. The site seemed to be deserted, and so I simply picked up the bucket by its filthy handle and hurried home, trying not to look overly suspicious. The whole episode was actually quite thrilling. After washing the muck off the bucket in the bathtub, I placed it in front of the window, knowing full well that later that evening I would be urinating into it. As you can see, I meant business, and I did not intend to miss anything.

I then turned off the lights, which at night would render me invisible to any fellow spectators, closed my own blinds, and then gingerly lifted one slat and began to watch. That first night little happened. In D14 the curtains were only half drawn, and I watched it intently. Unfortunately my field of vision was incomplete as that apartment was a couple of floors above me and from the angle I could see the occupants, a twenty-something couple, only when they stood up and walked about. They may have been having sex, but there was no way to be sure. They were definitely clothed from the waist up. I jotted the details into my notebook and went to bed. Things continued in this disappointing fashion for some weeks afterward—a flash of bare skin while changing, perhaps a quick grope before moving out of view, talking on the telephone with

R. T. BARNES

a variety of expressions. The problem was that the really interesting and shocking things had to be going on behind the closed curtains. And so even if the occupants had neglected to close the curtains or blinds all the way, it just did not reveal enough. All of that would change though, and when it did I certainly felt the fool.

One night I focused intently on a large crack in the curtains of C8, feeling that I might be getting close to something good. After all, there was excellent space to see through, I would estimate at least three inches, and I did have the higher ground, which afforded me the best possible angle from which to survey the room. Any military officer will tell you that gaining the higher ground is crucial to success.

I saw a flash of bare skin, and as I then reached for my cup of coffee, I accidentally knocked it onto my lap, scalding myself and dropping the binoculars at the same time. I froze for a moment, deciding whether to clean up the mess or continue spying. I picked up the binoculars—I didn't want to miss anything—but something had happened to them when they had dropped to the floor; some function had been switched on, something I hadn't noticed on the box. Now when I looked through them, all was bathed in an eerie green light. And I could see through the curtains and blinds. Every room was laid bare for me, all in ghostly green glow. Obviously these binoculars had some infrared function that had been activated when I dropped them. Where was the box? Unfortunately, it had gone in the recycling weeks ago. No matter, I had discovered the new function, and my hands shook as I gloried in my power. There in C8, right in the living room, on the couch, an elderly man was receiving fellatio from a much younger and more vigorous woman. The old man showed little expression in his face until the very end, about five minutes later, when he appeared to be having a mild stroke. He composed himself after a few moments and handed the young woman a few bills, hundreds I would imagine, and she abruptly left. I noted the details and time in my record book. Very little happened during the rest of the evening, just people watching television, making tea, going off to bed. At three AM I retired but could barely sleep—I was on my way! I was very weary at work the next day and most preoccupied. I could not stop thinking of green light.

The next night was even better. A14, F6, and D11 all featured full orgies, with a minimum of fourteen individuals each. A full third of the other windows featured smaller orgies of three to five perverts. Not only that, but some of the people switched between rooms. Apparently they all knew each other. What most shocked me was that they moved between rooms completely naked. Hadn't anyone noticed naked glistening perverts wandering the hall between orgies?

It was all as I had predicted. Here, finally, was the evidence. I recorded each detail in my book. I won't go into those details now, it's too obscene, but I'm sure anyone that has casually browsed Internet porn can imagine the bacchanalian goings-on. And now I knew. I knew that people really were behaving in this way, that it wasn't all some sort of media hallucination, that the infidelity statistics were, if anything, underestimating the phenomena. Yes, people were even worse than I had imagined. A horrible realization came to me. I had obviously been kept in the dark about the true cultural extent of the perversion. I'd been kept out of the club. As I rode the bus in the morning, they knew that I had not been to their orgies. They gave me knowing smiles. They judged me.

I suppose I should just admit the obvious—I'm just as flawed and bad and perverted as society at large. I wanted to see the wicked things because I felt the same primitive, carnal pull as any other flesh and bone human. I am reconciled to that. I have no problem with it. And I will say this—I was deeply hurt that no one, not even my acquaintances at work, ever bothered to let me know what was happening. Perhaps I'm simply not attractive enough.

The next night before beginning my usual surveillance at home, I put the binoculars in my coat pocket and went out for a walk. When there was no one else on the street, I would pull out the binoculars and steal furtive glances into the windows. Behind every window, bathed in beautiful green light, was a sex act of some kind and often an orgy. Every night, it seemed all of humanity went home, covered themselves in oil, and performed every imaginable act upon themselves and their neighbors.

When I returned home to my post, I saw that a dozen apartments were already swarming with naked bodies, with new arrivals by the minute. Soon the rooms became so crowded that the bodies were heaped in rows upon each other, with anonymous limbs that protruded from the mass, that shook frenziedly. By midnight, all of the orgy rooms were literally full from floor to ceiling and bodies so stressed the glass that several panes exploded outward with bodies tumbling to the street below. The orgies continued unabated. Perhaps they were so consumed with pleasure that they did not notice people tumbling down; in fact, the steady flow of bodies continued pouring from the window until the orgy mass had reached below window level. Looking down, I noticed that I hadn't even touched my tuna sandwiches or coffee. With a shaking hand, I quickly jotted down the event in my record book and then went to bed nauseous, waiting for the sirens to sound. After several hours I gave up listening; I drank seven NeoCitran packages and soon fell asleep.

In the morning it was as if nothing had happened. No broken bodies on the sidewalk, no blood, not even any broken glass. The apartment windows had already been replaced. Things went on normally on the street below; buses ran, cars honked impatiently, human beings scampered about on their way here and there. I ran down to the corner store and bought the day's paper. Nothing on the front page, nothing on page 2, no mention of the terrible event at all. Obviously it was all to be a secret. Things had gotten out of hand last night, and so it had all been tidied up, quickly and efficiently. There were people who were not to know about this. I was not supposed to know about this. I determined to sew my mouth shut and be inconspicuous. After all, what could I do? Those were consenting adults, and I am not their keeper. I went to work. Of course, at night all of my coworkers were constantly engaged in multiple-partner sex, my investigations had borne that out. I may well have been the only person in the city who was not a part of it. For some reason I was not to know. Why had I been kept in the dark? What would happen if I took one of my coworkers aside and said, "I know. I know what goes on at night. I could bring my own oil." Would that place me in some sort of danger? I spoke little and smiled until my jaw hurt. I didn't think that I had aroused any suspicion. On my way home I kept my eyes down. The binoculars had somehow affected my regular vision, and everyone's faces were bathed in green light.

That night I witnessed more orgies, less vigorous this time and in only a few windows. It was F11 where the real action was. A pyramid of finely cut stone lay in the middle of the room, surrounded by candles which supplied the only light. Soon a man entered wearing just a loincloth and holding a large round drum upon which he beat a slow, regular rhythm. I thought that I could almost hear it from my post. Then five other men entered, one of them being carried by the others. All wore loincloths. The four placed the one onto the pyramid and held down his arms and legs. The drummer's pace quickened. Having recently read a history of Mesoamerica, I immediately recognized the next figure to appear. Judging from his elaborate feathered headdress and accessories of jade and gold, this was probably an Aztec priest. In his hand he held an obsidian blade. He approached the man on the pyramid and deftly carved open his chest cavity and reached in for the still-beating heart, which he then held over his head, babbling as if in rapture. Next he would perform a ceremonial burning of the organ upon a golden dish.

I had seen enough. Whatever other horrors this city had to hide, I would let it have them. I was done, I had seen more than I had ever expected. I'd seen through those many windows directly into the dark heart of humanity. Let them have their wicked secrets! Perhaps, I told myself, not every city was like this. I would leave and take the binoculars with me; and if the next city was the same, then I would continue to the next, and then the next. No matter how long it took, I would find someplace that I could live in peace, someplace where I could look into a window and find people behaving not as animals. For just a moment, I glanced back at the windows and saw that every curtain and blind was open, each window was full of expressionless green faces. They were staring at me. And then I could hear the drums. The Aztec priest led a procession of my loincloth-clad neighbors across the street to the steps of my own building. They were coming for me! I was the next sacrifice! It explained the secrecy! They wanted my strong heart!

I took nothing but the clothes on my back. I fled out from the alley door and didn't look back. I'd forgotten to bring the binoculars, but it was too late. I fled into the night, not stopping until the sounds of the drums were far behind and then gone entirely. I fled into the woods.

The New Shirt

B RANDON HAD NEVER been attractive until he bought his new shirt. It was a simple shirt, light blue, button-down collar, and long sleeves. In all respects it seemed to be a typical dress shirt. Brandon had never felt any excitement when shopping for clothing because for his entire life nothing had ever looked good on him.

He noticed a change the first time he wore his new shirt in public. A woman smiled at him on the bus during his commute to work the next morning. At work his female coworkers were friendly and even, he suspected, flirtatious, which had never happened before. The next day he wore one of his old shirts and none of the women so much as looked at him, and when he tried to engage them in conversation, they were cold and unfriendly. He wore his new shirt again the next day, and once again, he was greeted with smiles and flirtation.

It was strange, Brandon thought, because the new shirt didn't seem any different from his other shirts. It was bland and conservative. Clearly there was some sort of special quality about it, something not immediately apparent, something secret and mysterious. Also, the shirt seemed to be sensitive to some people. When certain coworkers neared the shirt, its fabric would begin to emanate an unsettling scream, muted from a distance but growing in intensity as the person neared. Brandon found himself bolting from the room every time he felt the initial vibrations that announced the coming of a terrified wail. He would have to spend several minutes patting it reassuringly and whispering things like, "It's okay, nobody will hurt you." Brandon was very confused by his new shirt.

After having worn the shirt a dozen times, he realized the cause of the shirt's distress. It was racist. The shirt's fear began at the first sight of any person of any ethnic background other than Caucasian.

Brandon's coworkers assumed that he had learned ventriloquism and were offended by what they deemed to be his offensive and annoying practical joke. They did not realize that it was a racial issue, and so Brandon was only given a warning by his supervisor and then shunned socially by the group at large. He stopped wearing the shirt to work and would only chance it on evenings out. He had been increasingly frequenting dance clubs and other bars, where he discovered that his shirt made it easy for him to enjoy one-night stands, as long as his conquests were white. He regretted his shirt's unfortunate and backward attitude toward the other races—Brandon was not the least bit racist himself and considered all people to be brothers and sisters in humanity—yet still, he saw the sexual conquests as a major personal victory and took great pride and pleasure in this. Of course, he regretted that it was impossible for him to form any long-term relationship unless he wore his shirt every time his mate saw him. It was just not practical, and beside, he did not want to put the shirt under the stress of constant wear and washing—he intended to keep it looking good for as long as possible.

Unfortunately, in the large city in which he lived, it was difficult to avoid the various other races. After receiving several severe beatings, all accompanied by his shirt's piteous wailing, which was attributed to Brandon himself, he knew it was time to make a move.

After long consideration, he decided, as much as it offended his sensibilities to do so, to join a white supremacist compound in Arizona. It was called the Purity Ranch. Brandon had read about it in an exposé in one of the many left-wing blogs that he regularly read. Although the people of the Purity Ranch held racial views that differed radically from his own, in other respects they seemed less threatening. For one, they were not skinheads, and he would not have to shave his head. Also, they were pacifists, and their mission statement was that they simply wished to be left alone, and that no blacks, Mexicans, or Jews were allowed. Although no other races were mentioned, such as Asians or Arabs, Brandon assumed that they were not welcome either.

Brandon recognized that his shirt had changed everything. It was time to adapt. He quit his job and packed up all of his things into his van and drove to the Purity Ranch to start a new life. He hoped that he would find a suitable mate in this safe environment, one that would adore him for one or two days a week and tolerate him for the remainder. Brandon had saved a considerable nest egg, which he was confident would help balance the sublime attractiveness of the shirt with his own shortcomings.

Brandon was welcomed at the Purity Ranch, and because he was wearing his new shirt, he received many compliments on how handsome he looked. He noted several attractive young white supremacists and felt encouraged. After having made a generous contribution to the communal agricultural, septic, and activities funds, he was given a nice cabin of his own.

The next night he attended the weekly Purity barn dance. Once again he wore his new shirt and received much attention. One young flaxen-haired woman, daughter of the mayor of the Purity Ranch, payed particular attention to him; and by the end of the night he found himself deep in conversation with her. As they were about to leave together for his cabin, a dark-haired woman, who had been watching him admiringly throughout the evening, began to approach. To Brandon's utter shock and dismay, his new shirt began to quiver and sob. By the time this woman had reached him, the shirt was producing a high-pitched squeal. The woman fled to the corner and sipped at her peach cider nervously, at which point the screaming subsided. Everyone had stopped dancing and chatting, and now they stared at Brandon.

Seeing no other way out and feeling that these people would be sympathetic to his predicament, he explained everything. "But why then," the mayor of the Purity Ranch asked, "is it afraid of Annie-Mae?" Annie-Mae then broke down into tears and confessed that she was one quarter Jewish.

Brandon's new shirt was stripped from him, and thereafter the people of the Purity Ranch worshiped and revered it. It was placed in a glass cube and kept on an altar in the church. All future recruits would be put to the shirt test, and thus purity would be assured. Brandon, his hope shattered, spent the rest of his life in the cabin, rarely venturing out. Annie-Mae was driven from town and thereafter lived as a wild woman in the desert.

Of course, eventually a global plague killed off all of humanity and then Brandon's new shirt simply succumbed to neglect, it's fabric moldering and its seams failing. In due time, like everything else in the universe, it decayed into diffuse energy.

R. T. BARNES

Twin Pandas

I PROBABLY SHOULD HAVE breast-fed Annie when she was a wee little baby. Angel actually, she was such a little angel, and that's what I call her mostly. But I should have nursed her. They say the natural method is the best—makes 'em healthier and probably helps their little brains to develop properly. Don't get me wrong, there is something gross about having a little creature, even my little angel, sucking and slurping milk from a tit. It's almost like *incest* when you think about it. No, I went the way of the formula bottle, and I'm the first to admit that I should have just gritted my teeth and attached Annie to my humps like a good Christian. It might have averted a whole world of problems.

Now, you understand that this is all just between you and me, sweetheart. Lord only knows how much press it'd be worth if my private thoughts were to be known. There are people out there who'd actually sell this stuff, mothers who'd do it. Well, you'll never see that happen on my account. I mean, my story is worth as much as anyone else's, probably more, but I'd never sell out my little angel. So keep it zipped.

Of course, I support Annie in everything. I remember the first time she ever danced in the living room of the old rancher to a Taco Bell commercial. She was a natural. At six years old she could shake those hips like the best dancer in a Beverly Hills gentleman's club. The next day I had her in Ms. Bateman's school of dance; it was damned expensive, four hundred dollars a month, but I could tell how much she wanted it so we cut back on a few things. Well, most things. We couldn't deny *her* the American dream. It was just nonstop after that. Classes for singing and cheerleading too. She just got herself onto that A-train to stardom and never looked back. Even then she had that steely look in her eye, that cold stare of the champion. Well, it took her a while to really get those eyes all the time. She went on being a silly girl for a while, actin' goofy and like she didn't want to reach out and take a hold of that brass ring, the dream. We called all the parents of those dummies from school that kept distracting her and told 'em where to go, and the little bitches too; but it wasn't until I enrolled her in performance boot camp that she started to look at me that way, with those cold eyes, those almost murderous eyes, champion's eyes. Of course she wanted to go, as far as I remember it was all her idea. I'm sure it was her idea. I have to say it was a relief as we were all worried about possible muffin tops forming on her tum tum. A nine-year-old can't afford that kind of setback, not when there's a billion other little girls just ready to slit your throat with their perfectly manicured fingers. If you doubt me, just go to the Prettiest Lil' Darlin' in Grange County Pageant and you'll find out for yourself. Most of the Lil' Darlin's end up sucking like vacuums for their dinners in Vegas—I've heard a lot of stories about all that. Only the very best and brightest rise to the top, just like my little angel did. Oh, she went on and on about all the "awful things they did to me, Mama," just like kids do, but I know she's grateful to me now.

Annie wasn't the easiest child to rear up. As I said, she had those cold eyes. The eyes of a champion, sure, but it can be a bit unsettling sometimes, like when you wonder if she might hire some junkie to break into your house and rape and murder you. Probably with a knife, 'cause it would hurt more. What really gets stuck in my craw about the present state of our relationship is that everything I did, I did for her. I'll say it again, this was her choice, and what kind of a mother would I be if I didn't help my angel to be everything she could? Lord knows I wouldn't mind being in her shoes right now. I don't have the big houses, even though I'm owed at least that much. I don't have the big fat bank account. Well, I guess it's not so fat as it used to be, and it's only one big house now, but all the same, you got to show respect for the people that care about you, and you have to care for them as well. I mean, a card on every Mother's Day is nice and thoughtful, but it doesn't exactly replace my Prada handbag when it starts to look like an imitation Prada handbag. How could my little angel let me fall so far? Her own mother. Especially when times have gotten tougher and she ought to be surrounding herself with the folks that know how to keep and maintain a winner, which is what she *used* to be. I know that with my love and care she could climb the ladder again and we could go for tea and scones in Beverly Hills together and chat about JT and maybe he'd even come over to a party again, just like when my angel knew how to make a buck. Then she wouldn't need those cock-sucking lawyers to send me goddamned pieces of paper telling me what I can and can't do and where I can and can't go. And after all this, after our long road to the top together, after all the pageants, photo shoots, auditions, I was there for every single one, not to mention that as her former manager I was responsible for the whole turkey dinner. I remember her first record deal, when we sat in the office of that nice and very powerful executive (not to mention handsome for a man of his years and girth), and I couldn't believe the way he looked at her, as if she was some kind of golden idol out of the Bible. I knew we were gonna make it then, the way he looked at her told me so. Being a good mother, I took him to one side after we signed the papers and gave him a good old warning, "Not until she's sixteen, do you hear me?" He got the point. You've got to protect your kin 'cause no one else is likely to. But he was a decent type after all and very, very well-to-do. If she'd managed to keep her figure, she'd still have a husband. Damn, I wouldn't have felt hard done by if he were *my* husband. Wouldn't you know that she's poisoned him against me, and now he won't even take my calls. I can't imagine the things that little bitch told him. My angel, I mean.

And so what if we had to move the schedule up by a year or so. You buy a house, you've got to make a down payment, am I right? Damn hell

I am. And she only had to sleep with the one executive, and a handsome one at that. When I was back in my champion age, I had to do some very ugly things with six or seven agents. Thankfully that was well before the Internet. And what did I get for all that work? One lousy TV movie called *The Fool's Gold*, about a single mother raising a retarded boy who lays golden eggs. I couldn't get a bite after that and had to move back home and get that job plucking chickens. At least the woman I played in the movie, Christine Weatherwell, got rich. That should have been just the start for me—I was good, no matter what anyone says. I was like sunshine.

I'm sure you've heard about the latest news involving my angel. I know, it ain't natural. Of course it's all the rage these days to get an exotic child, and it certainly has done wonders for Angelina and Madonna, but being inseminated or whatever it's called with twin panda bear eggs is not natural. It sure ain't in the Bible. I'll say this for my angel, she sure does know how to keep a secret. All those months of being preggers and keeping the surprise right till the end, that does make me proud. I know my angel, and I know that she had a plan—she wanted to wait until she gave birth to those two adorable and endangered little cubs. She wanted to wait for the money shot, which is the DVD of my panda grandchildren exiting the baby tunnel. As I understand it, *Annie Does Pandas* is selling real steady, and she might be looking at a two-house career again soon. Yes, it's unnatural and an abomination and all that, but businesswise, it's tight. It's got the cameras back on her again, and I heard she might even be up for a couple of big parts. She'll be back on top again soon. Let her know how much I miss her, will you? Could you tell her that I'm wearing the same dresses and shoes that I was wearing two years ago? Could you tell her that I'm here for her, to help guide her through this new phase in her career?

Now, don't get me wrong—the situation is not right. I don't approve. Is it true that she's breast-feeding those pandas?

R. T. BARNES

The Lindbergh Baby

MY PARENTS WERE born without hands or feet and were warned that any offspring was almost certain to be cursed with the same affliction. The small town where they were both born, lived their whole lives, had me, and where I now live again in my old age, has a long history of missing extremities. To be missing a limb in this town is nothing special at all. Most of the townsfolk are missing a hand or foot, or at least a finger or two. Nobody knows why this is so. The water and air have been tested and are within reasonable levels of mutation-causing agents. It's just the way things are around here, I guess. I have all of my extremities, which makes me a bit of a freak.

My parents weren't considered to be freaks, but the fact that they had no extremities at all, except for their heads, of course, did make them a little odd. They were born within a week of each other, and neither one having hands or feet made them a perfect match. A match made in heaven, you might say.

I was different. When I was six I tried to chop off my big toe with a butter knife, but predictably did nothing more than than break the skin and frighten my parents. The dressing of the wound was a long process, as the gauze kept getting caught on their hand hooks and teeth.

I felt like a god in those days. I could do everything so much faster than my parents—no fumbling with coffee cups and the inevitable scalding; zippers, buttons, remote controls, cutlery were all simple matters for me. My parents needed more help than I did. I didn't need much help at all.

I'm not saying that my parents weren't good people, or that they didn't do their best or weren't loving. They were loving. They were wonderful parents. It's just that they didn't have hands or feet. All of the other children at school had parents with at least a hand between them. I fantasized about how much easier life must have been for the children with more fully limbed parents, how much quicker the breakfast must be; that Christmas and birthday presents would be wrapped with much greater precision, with the paper tight to the toy box, the tape flush across the seam, the corners sharp and crisp.

As I have said, I had wonderful parents. But I did feel as if I lacked in attention somewhat. Everything that they did took so much time. Have you ever tried to comb your hair with a hook hand? How about flip a pancake? Fold laundry. They were very busy. Of course, I would help them as much as they would allow, such as bringing Dad a beer on Sunday afternoon while he watched the football. But they were so exhausted from the constant struggle to perform even the most mundane of tasks that there just wasn't a lot of energy leftover for me. I'm not being a crybaby about it; these are just the facts.

On the evening of March 1, 1932, twenty-month-old Charles Augustus Lindbergh Jr. was abducted by an intruder from his crib. It was big news. It was the "crime of the century." I was six years of age at the time, and I could not fail to notice all of the attention this child was garnering. I wanted attention too, and so I hastily wrote down a ransom note, something to the extent of "Forty dollars on the front porch by five PM, or the kid gets it," and left it on the kitchen table as my parents attempted to fold a newly washed bedsheet in the laundry room. Then I ran out into the woods, which our little house bordered on, and hid myself in the lower branches of a pine tree and waited. I had only gone in about ten feet and could clearly see the house and my father as he tottered out into the backyard on his artificial wooden feet and called out my name. I remember the terrified tone of his voice; it frightened me but also gave me a feeling of power, the kind of power that a child should not exercise over one's parents. A diseased power. As soon as he neared the tree line, I threw myself to the ground and played dead. Dad carried me back to the house, careful not to stab me with his hooks, and both he and mother fawned over me for the next couple of weeks, but things soon returned to their normal course. They had never believed that I had actually been kidnapped. After all, the letter was in my own childish script.

Father became obsessed with a new hobby, attempting to put one of those little handcrafted ships into a bottle. Handcrafted is one thing, hook crafted is another. Even with Mother's constant support and aid, this was an extremely time-consuming project. I suppose he was trying to prove something to himself. I feigned kidnapping another twelve times by the time I graduated from high school. Eventually, my parents nicknamed me the Lindbergh Baby, and not without some affection, I would like to think. Other than these details, my childhood was fairly typical.

I left for college at seventeen and graduated four years later with a degree in engineering. I then moved to Capital City and began working for the city. I wrote home regularly and visited each Christmas. One year I walked into the house and found an almost illegible note written on the counter. After some time of examining the crude series of ink scratches upon the paper, my heart suddenly stopped. It was a ransom note. I ran into the backyard and there were my parents, sitting on the lower branches of that same tree that I had hidden in all those years ago. They were laughing hysterically, and then I joined in with them. It was funny. Childish but funny. That became a Christmas tradition for many years, right up until the time they both died in a car accident. The state should never have allowed my father a driver's license, and perhaps I should have sued afterward, as it might have been quite a lucrative case. Oh well, water under the bridge . . . They were in their early sixties when the accident happened. They left the house full of poorly constructed, half-finished ships in bottles, or ships partially in a bottle.

Eventually, I met Marie. She was a secretary at the sewage department. I can't recall now how I met her. She had lost her pinkie toe in a childhood bicycle accident. Her foot had gotten all tangled up with the chain while she was riding barefoot downhill, and her poor little toe had gotten all mashed up and had to be amputated. She showed me sketches of the toe that she had drawn from memory while in art school, and I praised her technical skill. We married after six months of dating. Nothing much special happened over the course of the next twenty years. We got along well; the sex was generally good while we still had an interest in it.

Eventually she reacquired an interest in art, as a midlife crisis of course, and began painting and drawing again, taking night classes and going to local galleries. I had taken an interest in my father's old hobby, ships in bottles. It was a tedious process, which I'm not sure that I enjoyed very much, but it did give me something to do at night and on weekends. I didn't find it all that difficult, what with having two fully functional hands. I asked Marie to do a few sketches of my first ship in a bottle so that I could have them framed and hung throughout the house, as a celebration of our talents, a symbol of our cohesion as a married unit. You should know that we never had children, and so we had plenty of free time for these kinds of things.

As it turns out, Marie had met some artist or other at a gallery and soon after informed me that she would be leaving in a few days. It seemed strange to announce that she was leaving before she actually did. Wouldn't it be better to simply say you were leaving and then do it right then? Much less uncomfortable for everyone. Anyway, it wasn't anything personal she said, just a small constant sense that her life wasn't worth living. It wasn't my fault, she said, pretty much everyone else lived empty, boring lives as well, and it wasn't such a bad thing if you could stand it. She said that she was under no illusions, that she realized that living with a city bus driver who painted at night would probably be just as dull, but at least it would be a different dull. And she realized that she herself was dull, that the most interesting thing about her was that she had shredded a toe off from her foot as a child; no matter, she was going to make the best of it. She had to.

I waited until she went into the bathroom and then I quickly wrote a ransom note and hid in a bush in the backyard. It wasn't premeditated; I didn't even think about what I was doing, it was all instinct. As for her, she didn't come out looking for me, didn't seem concerned at all, and she just shouted from the deck, "Who do you think you are? The goddamned Lindbergh baby?" Working on instinct again, I threw myself to the ground and played dead. That was the end of Marie. I'm sure she went on to an acceptable life, and if she's still alive, I'd like to think that she still paints pictures of fruit in bowls and landscapes and just maybe the odd mutilated toe.

Life didn't change much after Marie left. I worked Monday to Friday. I woke up at six AM, drank a cup of decaffeinated coffee (I can get a little squirrelly on the caffeine), ate two pieces of whole wheat toast with plum jam, off to work at seven and home by five thirty. Then TV and, occasionally, ship in a bottle. I retired at sixty-five and moved back to my parents' old house. I'd been renting it to my distant cousin Reggie for below market value since my parents' death. Reggie has only one foot but both hands—hands that he used to chop down the old tree that I used to climb into when I was "kidnapped." He hadn't even asked, just chopped it down and made a crude bench for the backyard and several prosthetic feet for himself. I will never forgive him for that, and he certainly isn't getting his deposit back.

I'm an old man now. I don't move very well. Nothing much seemed to happen in my life. It makes me sad to think of. I can't really remember much about the whole thing. The old kidnap tree is gone, and so I'm lying on the damp morning undergrowth behind the house. I didn't run out here; I walked out slowly, favoring the left side of my hip, which is riddled with arthritis. I got down gingerly; again, everything is sore these days. I don't know how long I'll lie out here, maybe forever. I could be devoured by wild wolves. Apparently they've been seen in these parts lately. I don't expect any visitors, but if someone were to break into my home, to steal things to support a drug addiction most likely, they would find a note on the kitchen counter, and the note would say, "Forty bucks on the front porch by five PM, or the kid gets it."

Mortality

Y EAH, SO ALL this stuff that happened today really made me feel not right and a little confused. I was strolling along singing that song from the commercial about the pill that cures antisocial urges 'cause it makes you not want to do it anymore. I mean steal and stab people and stuff, which is cool 'cause some people could need it, I can understand that. You know the song, it goes,

> What a weight off my back! da da da da da
> Now I'll never go back! da da da da da
> I've got my dog and cat! da da da da da
> I've got my Tolerex
> And I'm doing fine!
> OOOMPH

So you know the song I was singing. Anyhow, I'm just minding my own business, which is just natural for me, as you know I'm not wild about other people. Well, people I don't know or don't know very well; and I'll just add that I don't like crowds at all, but anyway, I walk past this house with an ambulance in front and there's these EMT guys carrying this dried-out old corpse on a stretcher from the house. I could tell the corpse was dead 'cause it just had this dried-out-corpse look, you know the one. So it got me thinking about my Grams 'cause that's where I was headed 'cause I had to drop off some flowers from my mom as it was Grams's birthday today, and Mom doesn't like to go by 'cause she doesn't like the smell. So I had to go by even though I'm not wild about the smell, but I don't mind it even then 'cause Grams makes cookies if she knows I'm coming, and they're actually pretty good most of the time. Oh yeah, and sometimes she'll give me a few bucks and says not to tell Mom, which why the jebus would I do that? So anyway, I hoped that Grams wasn't dead when I got there. As you know I'm a young man still, thirty-five and a half, and people my age don't like to think about death too much 'cause you never know what could happen, like a bus or something hitting you or a weird disease; and I still have a lot to accomplish in my life, especially with only two more years before my doctorate, which you know I can do a lot of stuff with.

So then, while I'm walking past this corpse and the EMT guys are loading it up into the ambulance, this kid, like seven or something who looked like one of those cherubs from Valentine's Day, this kid runs up with a stick and pokes at the corpse with it, and the whole thing just goes up in this big puff. This big puff of dust and this wind comes up and blows it all up into this big cloud, and everyone starts coughing dried-up corpse dust, except for me 'cause I hightailed it superquick. You would have gone jebus in your pants if you'd seen how fast I moved. You know how fast my reflexes are; you've seen it before, like when we stole those new-style fireworks to put in the frogs, and the Russian guy chased us, and we thought maybe he was in the Russian mafia 'cause they all control the holopyrotechnics deal. And then the frogs didn't even blow up 'cause they were just holographs in their asses, but the whole thing looked kind of cool, and I was kind of okay after that we didn't blow up the frogs anyway.

So I was thinking all the rest of the way to Grams about the dust and what if she was all dried-up too, and then what am I supposed to do? Call the police and then I'm like stuck there with a dead lady and then the jebus patrol is gonna ask a bunch of questions and who knows? Maybe they think I had something to do with it, want to get her money; and what if she left me a jebus load of cash in her will, and then they're looking at me with that look 'cause they don't care who really did what, they just want to finish up and get high, am I right? And then plus we already had planned the championship game of Stratomatic Social Engineering League 2024 edition, and I'm not about to give up my crown for nothing. I mean, Grams is pretty okay and everything, I'm just saying.

So I get to Grams's and just let myself in with the key she makes me keep on my key chain 'cause of her knees, and she doesn't want to get up. There's the TV playing in there, and it's *Viper Island*, about the people that have to avoid the snakes or get bit, which is A-one jebus all right, and that's her favorite show, so I feel like everything's all right. So I go into the den, and there she is; I can see the back of her head over the top of the big comfy chair she watches shows in. I said, "Hoop ya, Grams." She didn't say nothing, but she can't hear anyway and it was kinda loud as normal; and so I just went to look for some cookies, but there weren't any. And then I knew maybe something was not on the okay. And it's cold in there too, and then in the den I see the window is wide open, and there's this cat on the sill, a big black cat called Jezebel, which Grams called her 'cause she said the cat was a slut. That's what we should call ladies that like to do it a lot, Jezzies. Jebus, huh?

So this cat jumps on Grams, and she goes up in a cloud of dust just like what happened earlier. And there's just this cat with dust all on its fur on the chair now, and I'm shaking 'cause I don't know what to do, and maybe I should clean the cat. How do you know what to do in that situation, what when you don't want to get involved or anything? You run, that's what. But it really got me thinking about my mortality.

Splendid Isolation

I PACED MYSELF WALKING up the steps, what with my heart the way it is these days. I was already feeling sick with the anticipation of one last encounter with my erstwhile mother-in-law. I knocked on the door and was greeted with a gurgled and terse "It's open."

I walked into the kind of sideshow scene that I'd grown accustomed to over the years. Mother Connaggy stood in the middle of the room, a room that had long ago been cleared of all obstacles—the chairs, tables, and couch all fitted snugly against the walls—so as not to impede the matron. She was encapsulated in what looked like a large wooden wheelbarrow. The structure, or more precisely *the vehicle*, had been built around her by Sonny Connaggy. It was a sturdy construct, as it would have to be in order to support the avalanche of those many sheets and slabs of fat. She alternately caressed and then dug her meaty hands into the mass and pulled it out to a length of several feet. She said conversationally, "My doctor says that my skin surface, square footage wise, is equal to that of seven sturdy Scotsmen."

I nodded, rubbing the left side of my chest.

Sonny Connaggy, a faun of a man, sat in the corner, neck arched back, staring into the forest beyond. It was a yearning look, as it always had been. I've always been amazed that he managed to build his mother's ark, what with his tiny, delicate fingers—fingers that seemed much more apt for the origami badgers that littered the tables and floor. I assume they were badgers, but they could be raccoons or something else entirely; I never asked. He is agile and quick, despite being in his fifties, as I am, and can still nimbly dodge a heavy snack time ham hock or fat-laden appendage and scurry under a table as quick as a schoolboy.

Mother Connaggy began to wiggle and squirm in her human wheelbarrow, the wood creaking in an alarming way and started to hoot and point at a specific spot two feet away. Sonny leapt up and landed upon the barrow handles, behind MC, then attempted to lift the handles as MC threw her mass forward. It was a sad and unsettling seesaw, which one could confidently predict would eventually end in tragic circumstances.

I declined to join in, citing my weak heart, taking a pill for evidence and watched. MC gurgled at me and then let out a shrill series of barely comprehensible words. "Look at you now! That's what you get, mister! Drinking and snorting! Drinking and snorting! Drinking and snorting!"

MC had for decades been living under the delusion that I was an inveterate alcoholic and drug abuser. It's likely that some character in a novel or movie reminded her of me in some way and then everything got all muddled for her. It could have been in a dream.

Ten minutes later, Sonny had managed to maneuver her to the desired spot, and she ceased her odd vocal outbursts and let her arms rest limply upon her mounds of flesh. Sonny went back to his post at the window. I didn't ask myself what was so much better about that spot than the other one, only two feet away. I had been through this routine before and no longer cared why MC did anything.

I was there to gather memories of my late wife, Gormal. Gormal is a Gaelic name, which means deep blue eye, which is a lovely translation; although the name itself, to most non-Gaelic ears, is horrifically unattractive. She did have deep blue eyes. Also, she was not at all like her mother—not morbidly obese, not shrill, not clinically insane.

I decided to get to the point—that was the one thing about the Connaggy house—once you went in, it was so difficult to ever get to the point or do what you intended. It was a place of redirection. And thus I stated, "If I may, you mentioned in your call a box of . . ."

I was interrupted by the cruel crack of Sonny's backyard steel trap. MC lifted her arms to the heavens and proclaimed, "You've got one, Sonny! Quick, finish it, Sonny, before it gets away!"

Sonny was out back in a flash. I followed, not so much out of interest but simply to get away from MC who was chanting in a low voice her earlier refrain, "Drinking and snorting, drinking and snorting, drinking and . . ." and so on.

Out back Sonny was standing in a victorious pose, chest out, hands on hips over a small deer struggling under the crushing grip of what looked like a giant mousetrap. Sonny had built the trap himself. I told him that it was possibly the most horrible thing I'd ever seen. He didn't reply, just reached down with his clever little hands and broke the helpless creature's neck. I fled inside before he could begin cleaning the body.

I approached MC from behind and said, "You mentioned a box of Gormie's things that I should . . ." MC began to hoot and howl and lifted her massive arms to point at the front door. Apparently someone was there. I sighed and answered the door. It was a syntho-system weight—control-diet deliveryman, with several months worth of synthetic individually wrapped meals, hundreds of square and rectangular boxes packed neatly and efficiently into five large containers. I signed the order, and then instructed the young man to place the cartons along the sides of the living room, not in the middle of the room, and certainly not in the kitchen, which was full of cured deer carcasses hanging from the ceiling. The deliveryman had been prepared to do just that until he caught sight of MC tottering and reeling, ever so slightly, eyes bulging, and hands unconsciously digging and pulling at her own stretchy skin; she suddenly focused upon the poor man as he was about to cross the threshold, and then she hooted and howled and pointed and then seemed to insist that he "drank and snorted." The deliveryman did not put one container in the house. He got right back into his truck and drove away, likely never to return. I could hardly blame him.

I cleared my throat and asked, "Do you remember calling me and mentioning a box of Gormie's things, precious things, things of sentimental value?" This she had done. It had been five years since my wife's death, and it was the first time I'd heard MC's voice since the funeral. I don't know if I was more surprised by the call itself or that she was capable of operating a phone. Sonny had likely done the actual dialling. After a string of African-tribesman-style throat clicks, she had informed me, quite matter of fact, "I have a box of Gormal's things. Oh, memories, so precious . . . memories . . . come to Mother Connaggy . . ." Then dial tone.

I hadn't thought of the funeral for some time, but her voice brought it all back. MC hadn't been able to fit with her wheelbarrow through he doors of the church and was forced to stand outside with the doors propped open, allowing freezing winter gusts to buffet the mourners. She relentlessly interrupted the eulogizers with cries like, "It's a mother's pain! Can't you see my pain? What planet are you people from, you animals, you cold hearts, can't you see a mother's pain?" or "Why did she shun me, her own mother, the life giver, the nourisher?" or "Oh, how I wish she could have seen me when I was thin!" The speakers were forced to ignore and talk over her, and the PA had to be turned up to small-venue adult-contemporary concert level.

Anyway, before MC could answer my question, if that had been her intent, Sonny came in through the front door with a carton of syntho-meals, and MC was transfixed and focused. Sonny opened the carton and threw a Salisbury steak with mashed potato and apple crumble substance frisbee style to his mother, who caught it with one hand, tore the lid off with the other, and gorged upon handfuls of syntho-matter.

This quasi-food delivery method continued in a seemingly endless loop, surely against the advice of the company's weight loss experts and almost certainly voiding any money-back guarantee.

As soon as one meal was finished, she would wave her arms wildly, as if in panic, and so Sonny had to aim not for her hand, but where her hand was going to be, which he did with expert flicks of his nymphlike wrists. He gave a satisfied nod after each complete pass and counted out loud; I believe he was trying to set a personal best.

At some point, I can't say how long it took. Sonny turned to me and flatly stated, "Mother needs your kidneys. Both of them." He threw another meal and said, "Fifteen." I sat in stunned silence for a moment before he continued, "We both know this is the right thing for all concerned, that so much pain and strife has been inflicted upon poor old Mother by an ungrateful and insolent daughter, God rest her soul, and an equally egregious son-in-law. Although we both know that if there is any true blame for the long periods of estrangement, it lies with you, you who pulled the strings behind the scenes, you who never once called Mother 'Mother,' as if she were not your own flesh and blood, which symbolically she truly is. The estrangement hurt Mother more than you could imagine. The oh-so-rare visits and phone calls. Silence is the coldest, most devastating weapon, and you both knew that, and you know that now. Would you deny her your organs?"

"Something is owed. Restitution is in order. And after all, is it such a sacrifice? You with your exhausted heart, made weak by years of abuse, would you really let your organs be strewn about to strangers or, worse, be wasted entirely? If you look deeply into yourself, into your spirit, the seed of humanity and decency that resides somewhere amongst your entrails, then I believe that you will understand that you want to give Mother your kidneys, just to see the smile on her face."

MC was not smiling then. She had stopped eating, discarded boxes piled up around her feet and in the giant wheelbarrow, with ashy particles, like fish scales, plastered to her cheeks and jowls. Dead eyes were fixed upon my midsection. I was afraid.

"Get him the box," she ordered Sonny, her voice low and dangerous. Sonny, in his silent and efficient, almost elegant way, slipped down the hall.

MC spoke, "Oh, have I told you that I had the most wonderful day this summer? Sonny, my dearest most loyal flesh and blood . . . Sonny waterproofed my *walker*, don't call it a wheelbarrow for your life, not like that bitch from the TV channel called it when she wanted to put me in her show. I tore a strip off her, let me tell you, and I'm not the sort who needs to be on TV anyway. I'm just not like that, but you know that already . . . Sonny waterproofed my *walker* and pushed me out into Lake Incisor, and there I floated for hours, deep in my thoughts and sipping brandy, at one with nature. I thought of you and Gormal and of how we are all so connected. That we are born and live and learn and grow as human beings, and also that we must all return to the earth one day . . . We are all a part of some mysterious universal energy . . . Oh, my dear, could you bring Mother another meal, can you find a meatball pizza? You needn't heat it, just bring it here."

And so I rooted about in the carton until I found a box with a picture of a yellowish circle with grayish lumps, and then I made a motion to toss it to her, but she gestured for me to come forward. "Bring it to me," she said. "Bring it over like a good little gentleman."

By the time her sausage fingers locked around my forearm, it was too late. I immediately recoiled and frantically shook my arm, but it was of no use—years of reflexively squeezing at her own abdominal flesh had apparently honed and strengthened MC's carpal muscles. She was like a vice. She was calm. "I don't intend to let you get away, my dear little guppy," she said. "Maybe now you wish you hadn't done all the you-know-what while you were married to my sweet Gorm. Where is your vigour now? Your precious pride? What kind of man can't fight off an old lady?"

I passively offered her the pizza, but she waved it away and continued speaking, "I floated about all day, and it was peaceful and beautiful, and I don't know if I've ever felt so alive and nurtured. When my legs got so cold that I could barely paddle myself back to the shore with my little footsies anymore, then Sonny, my dear Sonny, hitched a chain to my walker and pulled me up out of the water with his truck. And there I stood on the sand, all at peace with nature and the Holy Spirit . . ."

There was nothing for me to do but be cordial and wait for an opportunity to escape. "It sounds wonderful. I'm happy for your experience." To which she screamed back, "Leeches! You're happy for me? Really? You're happy for my legs to be covered with bloodsucking leeches? Well, thank you so much for your consideration, Mr. Thoughtful!" Her grip tightened, and I vomited into her wheelbarrow walker, the greenish liquid sloshing back and forth as MC recoiled, fell forward, and recoiled again and again. "Leeches!" she screamed.

Her grip tightened further still, and I heard something snap in my wrist, although I felt nothing because of the adrenaline rush, I suppose.

"Leeches, Mr. Happy, oh yes!"

Sonny had slipped up silently beside me, holding a shoe box neatly tied with chiffon ribbon. He threw the box into the corner, informing me that I would have it "after the procedure." He trotted back into the darkness of the hall and returned pushing a hospital gurney before him. He stopped behind MC and casually produced a syringe from his pocket, tapping the needle and squeezing the plunger to remove any bubbles. "Just a bit of general anesthetic," he said.

How do you believe, even in the face of the obvious, that people, even strange and sadistic people, could do something truly horrific, and not just horrific in a general sense, such as committing crimes against some anonymous person that you have never met and never would have and are usually quite plain looking to boot, but against yourself, that you are actually the focus of someone willing to do very bad things? It was clear that these people intended to remove my kidneys right then and there. This is what happens.

First comes shock.

Then fear.

Blinding, uncontrollable, explosive fear.

And that's what happened to me—I exploded. I exploded backward, away from the ark of flesh, from the python fingers, from the needle, hearing the grinding of my broken wristbones and Sonny's voice, "Don't worry, I have a surplus dialysis machine in the pantry," and then came the recoil, the recoil of my whole body as it shot back, a limp and helpless thing, back at MC, then the collision and the creaking of timbers as MC lurched forward and back, finally losing her footing and arched backward with arms flailing. And then the sharp cracks of multiple fractures as she went back all the way, splinters and large pieces of treated wood and forgotten snack treats exploded in all directions, leaving a cloud of sawdust and syntho particles. MC was under that cloud, a sharp accidental wooden stake protruding from approximately the location of her heart. Sonny was beneath her, simply crushed. I fled, shoe box in hand.

I thought of Sonny as I drove along the coniferous-lined routes away from the Connaggy house, and how he had looked so longingly at some unknown place in the wilderness. I understand it, the yearning for peace, and to be left alone, and to leave responsibilities to other men—men that want them or can live peaceably with them. Splendid isolation.

My arm and shoulder began to ache, and I knew what was coming and surrendered to it. When I awoke, to my horror on a hospital gurney, but with all organs intact, a nurse gave me the ribbon-tied shoe box, which a thoughtful EMT had rescued from the tangled remains of my vehicle. It seemed to her more of a miracle, and more pleasing, that the box had survived than I. In my weakened post-heart attack state, I was unable to undo the ribbon knot, and so the nurse did it for me. The nurse looked perplexed when she opened the lid, as the box contained nothing but empty spicy jalapeño nacho chip bags and fried chicken syntho-meal containers. She frowned and said, "I thought it'd be something good," as if I'd betrayed her. As if I'd led her to believe that there was much more to look forward to than there really was.

Glass

O LD JANE LIVED above a bakery and existed on nothing but fresh rye bread with garlic butter and powerful, bitter coffee. She hadn't been away from her street in so long that she never even thought about it anymore. She didn't have a television although her daughter had been promising her one for years, and so she spent her time reading novels or sleeping. Mary, her daughter, a skinny divorcee who had left her husband for a real estate agent, who as it turned out, just wanted to sell her a house, visited each Sunday to bring twenty-five dollars and tales of the infernal intrigues of her coworkers at the bank. "There's a novel there worth all the money in the vault," she often said. Old Jane tried her best to listen to the outcome of each petty affair or rivalry and was glad when her daughter said good-bye.

One night, a smooth little black stone put a perfect hole in her living room window and landed cradled between the pages of *A Lover for Loretta*, a borderline erotic tale of frontier romance. She sat for a moment in puzzlement, irate that there should be a hole in her window and amazed that the stone should fall with such grace upon her book. When she looked out to the street, it was empty but for a miserable German shepherd, skulking pathetically in the pouring rain. Old Jane used Saran Wrap and Scotch tape to seal the hole. She woke up early and found a puddle on the sill, as the rain had undermined the tape, drop by drop, while she dreamed of firm loaves of fresh rye bread.

She woke and ate several slices of rye bread ravenously. When she'd finished an entire pot of coffee, she brewed another, mixing old grounds with new, and determined it to be her bitterest brew ever.

In the afternoon, the rain intensified. She called a glass shop and had a man sent to make an estimate for a new window. He recoiled in disgust when he entered the apartment but said nothing of the acrid, garlicky atmosphere. Hardly glancing at the window, he announced, "Five hundred." Then after allowing himself a slight breath, he said, "And not until tomorrow." He fled without waiting for a response, not bothering to close the door behind him.

That same day she bought duct tape, after many assurances from the teller that it was absolutely impervious to moisture, and applied it to the window. Her daughter agreed to finance the repair while rhythmically pointing out that it would delay a trip to Maui for which she claimed to have been saving for over four years. That night, another stone made another perfect hole in her window. There was not even a dog in the street to hold witness. The two holes were barely a foot apart, and Jane feared that another hole would shatter the glass completely. She stiffly swept up the little shards while keeping an eye on the street below. She found a smooth gray stone under the dining table and placed it on the windowsill, near its mate.

The rain continued. In the morning, Jane examined the duct tape and nodded in approval as it had held firm. She called the glass shop. "I don't want the window yet," she said. "Not until after the rain." The rains did not stop for two months, and in that time, the city stank with rot and chaos.

It was under that gray sky that Jane's daughter jumped from the top of her apartment building, wearing a wet tracksuit and a head filled with the knowledge that her story about bank workers was not worth all the money in the vault. Old Jane would never know that Mary had written the novel that she had so often talked of writing. Mary had received the one hundred and fiftieth and last rejection letter of her writing career, which had started and ended with a tedious account of bank life. The manuscript that had been so warmly nurtured and which had ultimately destroyed Mary had been left in a neat bundle tied together with a string on the kitchen table. The landlord had thrown it into the trash with the contents of the refrigerator and the many rejection letters. A new tenant was placed in the apartment the next day.

Old Jane was alone without the daughter she had never really liked very much and whom she'd always secretly feared might do something like jump off a building. She was distracted. There was little else for her to do but sit at the window and wait for someone to throw a stone at her. A slow, agonizing, reluctant realization came to her—not only was she left alone in the world, finally, but was also reduced to a poverty that seemed as inevitable as boredom. She was alone with government checks and bitter coffee to sustain her.

Old Jane resolved to effect one small wonder. She would prevent any further holes in her window. She sat at the window and drank her coffee and licked garlic butter off a dull blade, keeping to her task as patiently and steadily as a grave digger. But Old Jane's body betrayed her, and she cursed her ancient bowels, and when she couldn't hold it in any longer she shuffled off to the facilities. Of course, just then another stone struck. Hearing the tiny explosion, which she had been powerless to prevent, she exclaimed, "Oh, what have I done with my years?"

Stop and Go

D ROOL. THERE'S NOTHING I hate more than human drool. From an animal like a dog, that's disgusting enough, but from a person, it's beyond words. If there is any true dignity to the human spirit, then drool is its ebb tide. And I know something about drool. Human drool, specifically. I'll talk more about it later, but first we have to go over a few other details. I'll start with my high school reunion.

I was pleased that no one recognized me. I wouldn't have expected them to. Not in a ten-thousand-dollar suit, not with an additional fifty pounds of solid, hard-earned muscle. I wore an expensive and perfectly crafted nose, elegant yet masculine. I'd gone through hundreds of photos of male models, all with desirable noses, before I picked out the one that was just right for me, that fit my persona; again, elegant yet masculine. I know that my style is elegant yet masculine because I formed several focus groups to deal with the question of my style to make sure I had everything right. I enjoyed forming the focus group. It was a chance to absorb the simple wisdom of twenty representative samples of society, from the morbidly obese Southern grandmother to the twelve-year-old promising soccer player. Of course, they differed in many ways in regard to their own personal definition of what makes a man desirable to women and a cause of envy in other men. That was the title of the experiment, "Is Robert Buckman desirable to women and a cause of envy in other men? And to what extent?" A five-hundred-dollar prize for the best answers, which added a competitive edge and made the whole thing even more of a success than it would have been otherwise; although I'm sure it still would have been great.

I'm a wealthy man. Not Bill Gates well-to-do, but with millions to spare. I'm not bragging, it's just that I'm the kind of guy that needs to succeed, and I can thank high school for that.

As I've said, no one recognized me. I have little memory of most of my former schoolmates. Very few names, I can't remember much who belonged to which clique. I have a neutral opinion of the great majority. I had only two real friends back then, and most of the rest of the kids, several hundred, were more or less mannequins, or robots, that performed the duty of inhabiting my childhood world. I didn't know them, and they didn't know me. I had regular interactions with only two groups; my friends, Kenny and Paul, and the bullies, Brandon, Rufus, and Todd. Todd was the leader and primary antagonist, with the other two just as likely to be victimized as anyone else.

I made my money in the toilet business. My company, Stop and Go, installs coin-operated stand-alone public toilets on city streets. I've installed thousands of them, many in European capitals, where bodily functions are much more a part of the common culture. But it's really catching on in North America as well, but mostly in smaller cities and towns where they seem to be a bit of a tourist attraction. I've heard of people driving hundreds of miles just to go to a small town like Peacock, Kansas, for the pleasure of pumping seventy-five cents into the Stop and Go facility after having dinner at the Applebee's, which is right across the street. Great location.

Most people would assume that the most likely course to success for an unpopular nerd would lie in the field of engineering or computers. I wasn't that kind of nerd. I'm not sure that I was even a nerd at all, at least not in the classic sense. No pen protector, no coke-bottle glasses, no suspenders for my pants. I was just shy, that's all. I used to have a

R. T. BARNES

chronic sinus infection, and this did cause a lot of sniffling, and the occasional yellowish green booger dangling from a nostril. I used to daydream a lot about being an infantry man on the Russian side in the battle of Stalingrad (I was fascinated by that battle, as it was the ultimate in good versus evil, and everyone who fought the Nazis was good. The Nazis were evil, everyone knows that), and then I wouldn't notice anything until the teacher rapped his ruler on the front of my desk and told me to go to the washroom and clean off my face; and sometimes, if I'd been daydreaming particularly deeply, I'd have to clean the snot off my desk as well. As I've said, I had a chronic sinus infection.

After forty minutes at the reunion, I had not been approached once. This surprised me, as I was clearly the best-looking person there. I had not gone unnoticed, certainly not! I noticed many furtive glances. I was obviously cause for some interest, if not celebration, but perhaps it was just a case of intimidation on their part. Since I've graduated and become successful, I've had the time and means to make up for the lost years and pick up a few skills. Hence the black belt in karate, the sculpted physique. For the last six months I'd been training with a professional break dancer and decided to introduce myself with a little demonstration. There were a few couples dancing, but I soon had the floor to myself. The song was "Rockit" by Herbie Hancock, which was excellent as my training specialized in early eighties themes. My instructor repeatedly tried to push me in the direction of crunk, but I steadfastly refused—crunk was not part of the plan!

I must have been quite a sight, a full-grown man spinning recklessly on his back in the middle of a school gymnasium, wearing a finely tailored Italian suit, no less. When the song began to fade out and transition to "Careless Whisper" and my final spin slowed and stopped, allowing me to pose with my head perched cheerily on palm, reclined with clinical precision (I'm sure that none of the audience understood how much elbow grease it takes to make a demanding break dance routine look so effortless), I was pleased to see that a dance ring had formed around me and was clapping enthusiastically. High school meet the real Robert Buckman! Now that the ice had been broken, an attractive woman, midthirties, blonde bob, killer bod, approached and offered me a hand up. I didn't recognize her face and felt a moment of disappointment that she was not an old-school chum, so to speak, but probably a wife or a girlfriend. I decided this was just as well, as admiration from the outside surely brings admiration to the inside. I graciously accepted her offer.

"Robert Buckman," I offered.

"Alice Kessler," she replied. I could feel the blood drain from my face. "Todd's wife," she added, as if there was nothing wrong with being Todd Kessler's wife, as if every moment of life wasn't spent wrestling with the fight-or-flight instinct, as if she was not obsessively asking herself the same question, over and over again, "How can I hurt this man, Todd Kessler, really hurt him, bring him to his knees and force him to look up at his master, the one who has taken his pride away, and acknowledge that he is less, that he has been beaten?" It was odd, because she seemed so happy.

Alice Kessler should not have been happy. Once I'd become successful and had the time and means to dedicate myself to my physical and spiritual betterment, I'd started keeping tabs on old Todd. By means of a detective firm, Barry Slate Surveillance, I received a biannual report on the life and times of Todd Kessler, my enemy. Todd had become a loser; there's no other way to say it. Like so many other high-achieving school-athlete bullies before him, he had been unable to cope with the different problem set of the real world. He'd peaked in high school. His sheer physical size counted for little, post graduation. Oh yes, he did continue to bully, but there is little glamour to being the king of Supersave

Copy House or Fat Charlie's Car Wash and Soft Serve Ice Cream. And his bullying was confined to verbal threats and intimidation. After assaulting a teenage coworker at the Denim Hut, he served two months in the local correctional facility, had his wages garnished after the civil suit, and had to move back into his parents' house for several years. His life was a never-ending string of menial jobs, broken relationships, and alcohol dependence. He never strayed from our hometown. Perhaps he thought that if he hung in there long enough, then the universe might redeem him, like the usurped prince in a fairytale who is miraculously returned to the throne by fate. If that's the case, then someone should have taken pity and informed the poor man that fate is a myth and that in the real world nobody remembers the glory days of a worn-out old high school bully. Nobody cares, except for me.

Eventually the reports on Todd became tedious, always the same sob story. It was obvious that his future was already written for him, and so a couple of years ago, I informed Barry Slate that his services would no longer be needed. I thought I knew all I needed to know about Todd Kessler, and I was pleased.

Alice continued to beam her impossible smile at me. This was the moment I had been preparing for all these many long years. I had achieved everything that I had ever dreamed of, except for one last detail—shaming Todd Kessler and hopefully causing greater hopelessness and despair in his life. And if it ended in suicide . . . well, he's made his own bed.

"And where is Todd?" I asked. You might think that at this critical juncture that my heart rate would be increasing, my palms sweaty, that I might have a creeping anxiety. You would forgive me those reactions after such a long buildup. You would be wrong. After the initial shock of meeting Alice, I immediately began practicing breathing techniques that I had learned on a sabbatical in Cambodia. The ruins, by the way, are spectacular. Anyway, thanks to my training I was in full control of my body.

"Just wait here," she said. "I'll bring him over." I redoubled my breathing techniques. I'd not noticed Todd when I entered and had assumed that he was late or might not show up at all. Either way it didn't matter, as I'd planned to stay a few days anyway. There would be plenty of time to find Todd Kessler. Alice walked into a dark corner where I lost sight of her momentarily. She then emerged into the light with a man in a wheelchair. The figure wore sunglasses and appeared to be unconscious, his head swaying slightly, his chin resting on his chest. He wore a Dallas Cowboys football jersey and sweatpants. A thick string of drool hung from his pale lips and collected in a tin pot that had been jerry-rigged to his head with a coat hanger. So this was Todd Kessler?

"Todd isn't doing so well these days," Alice said.

"No, he doesn't seem well at all," I stammered. My breathing regimen collapsed, my pulse raced, I felt light-headed. "How?" I croaked.

"Nobody knows . . . the doctors sure don't. Just all of a sudden one morning I woke up and he was like this. Deaf, blind, mute, and quadriplegic. They hooked up some wires to his brain, and they say it's working just fine, and he's like a prisoner in his own body. He doesn't even know where he is right now, but he knows he's somewhere. Were you two good friends?"

"No, I wouldn't say good friends." No, I wasn't good friends with the man who had literally crucified me as a child. He crucified Kenny and Paul too. Todd and his two cronies, Brandon and Rufus, had built three sturdy crosses in shop class and dragged us out onto the soccer pitch and crucified us. It was all done with materials from shop class. There was no one else around because my friends and I had been stuffed into ball bags and dragged into the gym supply room until the school was empty. Then we were dragged out to the soccer field and one by one held down upon a wooden cross while metal pegs were hammered through our hands and feet, thus securing us to the crosses. Then each cross in turn was lifted and secured into a predug hole. When it was done, all Todd said was, "That's what you get for being a fag—Fuckman." As you know, my last name is Buckman. Todd often called me Fuckman, implying that I was a homosexual, which I am not. I've always assumed that Todd was a latent homosexual, and although Mr. Slate's investigation turned up nothing on that front, I still have my suspicions. Todd, after admiring his handiwork, surely the high point of his life to that point, turned and ran away, with the others close in tow. Brandon and Rufus weren't even laughing; they knew that they might be the next ones up on crosses. I'm sure that I don't need to describe the pain.

We were found ten minutes later by a homeless man, Gregory Austin Taylor, who had once been a university professor, an academic. I don't know if he's still alive. I hired Barry Slate to find him, but some people just can't be found. He was looking for discarded partially full juice boxes, as he often did on the school grounds after classes, when he came upon us. He shambled over to us and stared motionless for a few moments, perhaps wondering if we weren't some kind of school art project or a Christmas display maybe. He muttered the words "Sweet Jesus of Nazareth" and went running off. Five minutes later, an ambulance arrived with five police cars. Clearly, Gregory had alerted the authorities. That man is a hero, wherever he is now, alive or dead.

I was in hospital for two months after the incident. I recovered fully, with only minor nerve damage to my hands and feet. Kenny and Paul left the hospital soon after I did. Kenny had a limp, but Paul seemed fine. We didn't speak or play together much after we got out of the hospital. I suppose that we all saw each other as a potential magnet for more cruelty and violence. Of course, we don't talk or hang around at all anymore because they're both dead.

The episode didn't seem to cause that much of a stir within the school itself, at least not by the time I was back in classes. A few classmates offered quiet words of encouragement. Nobody made fun of us for being crucified. I would have gone with Jesus Junior, if I'd had to pick a suitably mocking nickname.

Gregory Austin Taylor was blamed for the crucifixion, against my protestations. Thank God he disappeared. Kenny and Paul went along with it—they were afraid of Todd. They needn't have been. Todd and his cronies went down that night for attempting to burgle Johnson's Jewellery Shack out on main street. They first broke into the shop next door and then smashed through the wall into the jewellery store, again using tools stolen from shop class. They didn't realize that the alarm system had been triggered despite their clever ploy. Rufus was shot dead by the first officer on the scene, who, in the dim light, mistook a hammer for a pistol. That seems a bit of a stretch to me, but then again, one shouldn't break into private businesses in the dead of night and expect sunshine and daisies. Todd and Brandon were given suspended sentences, and amid all of the ensuing fuss, their parents agreed with the prosecutor and judge that the boys should be sent to military academies, separate ones, until well after graduation. So I never saw any of those three again—not until the reunion.

Todd suddenly moaned. It was a low, stupid moan, the sound of an animal caught in trap. "Alice, are you sure he doesn't know what's going on?" It was difficult to pry my eyes from the mass of atrophied humanity that was now Todd Kessler.

"He can't hear, see, or talk. He just groans a little sometimes to let us know he's still alive." Alice spoke without pity, without pain, in the tone of someone who is used to caring for a cripple. I suppose it gets normal after a while. It was all too much for me. I felt ill, and it must have been plain on my face because Alice asked if I was okay.

"No, I must have come down with something. I've actually felt bad all day," I lied. She asked when I was leaving town and suggested that it might be good thing for Todd spirits to spend some time with me.

I replied, "But didn't you say that he has no idea what's going on around him?"

"Well, it couldn't hurt."

I told her that I'd be staying at my mother's place for a couple of more days, gave her my cell number, and said to call me in the morning. She smiled and rubbed my arm. I know what that means—it's a sexual cue, either conscious or subconscious, that invites further and increasing tests of sexual attraction. She was flirting with me. And right in front of her black hole of a husband. The fact that Todd was in his own little hell and oblivious to the fact, it did not make the moment any less delicious for me. I could have this woman—Todd's woman.

I could feel a palpable sense of relief as I left the gym, leaving all those regular people to their nice little mediocre lives. I suppose that I'm not really neutral in regard to my fellow graduates after all. I am neutral to their existence as former classmates, sure, but as typical human beings, they clearly leave something to be desired, as does the rest of the general population. I don't know, I suppose they're probably nice people, although at least a few are probably alcoholics or drug abusers. It's not important, they don't concern me.

I did not go to my mother's house. I'd lied to Alice about that. My mother isn't so wild about Bobby Buckman these days, and the feeling is mutual. For one thing, both her and my father, my dead father, never accepted that Todd and his cronies were responsible for the crucifixion. They were Jehovah's Witnesses. Apart from my own incredulity over their insane religion and vengeful god and my screaming fits that ensured I would not be forced to harass the community as a door-to-door zealot, my crucifixion was a blasphemy so extreme that their mere proximity to it would surely curse the family for generations to come. My father, in his severely starched white dress shirt, demanded, "Why didn't you fight back? How could you let a homeless wino damage us in this way? Where is your faith in God?"

"I don't think he's a wino. Todd did it anyway. Why don't you go over to Todd's house and kill him? God killed his own son. You're not even related to Todd!" That didn't go over very well. Later on Dad died for lack of a blood transfusion. He never got to see the end of the world, but I at least got to see the end of him. When I completely abandoned the faith after graduation, that was the end of my association with the Buckmans. If you're not in the faith, then you're not in the family. It's fine with me; I don't need outside help anymore, thank you very much.

So I stayed at the Hilton. That night I drank a bottle of wine before getting into bed, and even then I slept poorly. I dreamed that I was back on the cross again, and that Gregory Austin Taylor was before me, but instead of running for help, he held a mirror to my face. I didn't see myself in that mirror . . . it was Todd Kessler, as the blind, deaf, mute, quadriplegic that he had become. It gave me brief pause when I awoke, the meaning of the dream. Obviously, it meant that I had become some kind of cripple myself, an emotional cripple. I didn't waste too much time on the thought—it was bullshit. Todd Kessler had crucified me, and that fucker deserved whatever he got, and whatever was coming, although I couldn't imagine things being any worse. I ordered eggs Benedict from room service and ate it with gusto. I've always loved room service, even when the food isn't very good. I always feel like I'm on vacation when I stay in a hotel, even if the hotel is located in a shithole of a town.

Alice called me that morning and, with her incessantly cheerful tone, asked me over for breakfast. I agreed, although a small voice in the back of my brain warned me to stay away from the freak show. But the temptation of having Alice, preferably in front of Todd, was too much. I placed the breakfast tray outside of the door, with a ten-dollar tip tucked under the saltshaker, and drove to the Kessler home. It's a small town, too small to have a real ghetto, but north of Thirtieth Street was our hometown version. Certainly there were a few meth houses tucked away amongst the duplexes and ranchers. Houses there are generally small and mostly well kept, except for the odd ramshackle palace with the brown lawn and faded siding. On the whole, I wouldn't feel in danger walking these streets at night, but then I am a black belt in several disciplines.

Todd's house was of the brown lawn and faded siding variety, but then he didn't get around to much maintenance work anymore. Alice met me at the door in a nice little pink sundress, with her black bra straps showing. Another signal. I paced my breathing.

She sat me down at the kitchen table, across from Todd, globs of ropy saliva hanging from his chin. She gave me that vacant hick smile and told me that she knew what Todd had done to me. She said she wouldn't mind if I didn't want to get my own back on him. It was over quickly, up against the table, skirt up, panties down, her staring at Todd the whole while. When it was over, she emptied his overflowing drool pot into the sink and said I'd better go. And I did. Somehow I thought the scene might shake Todd out of his paralysis, that he might suddenly jump up and force me to kill him. He muttered a low groan as I left, and that was it. I guess she really did hate Todd after all.

I drove straight to the airport, leaving my bags at the hotel. I thought about Kenny and Paul and how they'd died in a far-off desert, their caskets sent home draped with flags, and if they'd ever gotten what they really wanted out of life.

Gorilla

I WAS VERY HAPPY. Things were going really well with Jean. We were hardly fighting at all, and sometimes we even laughed at each other's jokes. Several times we nodded in agreement at each other's profound observations—comments regarding the state of modern culture and/or our friends' personal lives. Well, truth be told, mostly just our friends' foolish decisions with regard to their relationships and careers. Of course, you can't tell your friends anything—they never listen. It's really best to just buy oneself a good sturdy writing pad and work out what they need to do, in the comfort of one's own home and without all of those annoying complaints. If you put that little notepad someplace safe and wait, then one day, on the odd chance that you are asked to be really, really honest, then you can pull out the file and strike while they're desperate. I think that it's a good idea to keep all of your friends' files well labeled, to avoid confusion over whose woes are whose.

Anyway, things were going great with Jean and me. It was my birthday, and I was very excited about what Jean was planning for me. I knew it would be something fantastic, what with how well our relationship was going. I love presents and surprises.

One the eve of my fortieth birthday I ran myself a nice warm bath with candles and some relaxing music, a medley of popular classical themes. I heard the front door open as I was applying a mixture of lavender and honey bath salts to the water. Abandoning the salts, I ran to the living room, all giddy with excitement and expectation, and clad in nothing more than a hastily thrown-on terry cloth towel! Young at heart!

Jean was standing in the living room, staring absently at a baby gorilla who was presently tearing one of our sofa cushions to shreds. Of course, I was speechless. With what seemed a great effort, she turned her gaze to me and spoke, "Happy birthday." She merely breathed the words, and I wondered if her asthma was acting up again.

"Well, it's not technically until tomorrow . . ."

"That's the problem. That's why I had to bring your present today because I won't be seeing you tomorrow on you birthday." Her words fell out of her mouth like lead. "I'm leaving you. Again. Do you like your present?"

"No, I do not. I mean, I suppose that it is thoughtful. I mean, I can't imagine the lengths you must have gone to, although I've never expressed any interest whatsoever in owning a gorilla . . . why are you leaving me?"

She paused, but just for a moment. "You're too predictable."

"I thought you liked that about me. You're always telling me what a 'stand-up guy' I am. I don't understand this at all. Are you in love with someone else?"

"Of course. And I just hope that you can find it in your heart not to resent me for it, or be passively aggressive to the ape like you are with me." With that she strode out the door, adding over her shoulder, "I'll be sending my brothers by for my things. Please don't make a scene with them, you know what they're like . . ." And then she was gone. I was left with nothing but a baby gorilla. Well, I still had my apartment and all of my things, as well as a healthy savings account. Thank goodness Jean and I weren't married.

But what of this baby gorilla? It had stopped tearing the cushions apart and was meekly licking a plastic apple as it reclined against the arm of the sofa. It stared at me. I felt it was judging me with those large and primitive eyes, asking the question that we both yearned for an answer to—what now?

It was only then that I noticed a terrible stench of feces emanating from it. "Are baby gorillas supposed to smell like feces?" I queried the creature. It stared back mutely. I decided that there was nothing for it but to sacrifice my own special birthday bath for the sake of a more pleasant-smelling gorilla. He didn't seem to mind it at all and was soon splashing and sloshing about and playing with my rubber ducks. I decided to call him Ducky—absolutely adorable, don't you think? He seemed to like the ducks very much, and so it was nice to find that we already had something in common. Later, after towelling off, we sat together on the couch and ate popcorn while watching *Sleepless in Seattle*. Ducky was very well behaved.

Ducky and I became best friends and did everything together. Every Sunday we went to the park and fed the ducks. That was always a good time, and it was so cute to see Ducky hand-feeding the bravest of the birds. Sometimes, very rarely and I think out of confusion, he would accidentally snap one of their necks. I didn't have the heart to stop taking him.

I brought him to my office once, and he was a big hit. I mean, how many people have a pet gorilla that they can bring to work? It was great fun to show him off, although some of my coworkers were clearly jealous. One party pooper even asked about the smell, even though we'd just had a bath that morning!

Of course, I knew that Ducky would get bigger, but he seemed such a gentle soul that I didn't worry too much about it. When he reached two hundred pounds, I hired a local high school dropout girl with braces and thick-rimmed glasses to babysit while I was at work. Ducky had been creating quite a mess at home while I was out, likely out of frustration that I wasn't there to watch movies with him. I assumed the babysitter would take care of that. I suspected that Laura, the babysitter, might be a drug addict; but with no one else willing to take the job, I reluctantly hired her.

On the first day I came home after work and found that Ducky had broken both of her legs and hidden her behind the couch. That was it, I knew that I had to lay down the law and show Ducky who was boss. "Not this time!" I shouted. I fixed Ducky with a stern, patriarchal gaze and said, "No hurt! No hurt!" It seemed to be a very tough and effective statement as I said it, and so I couldn't have been more surprised when Ducky reached out and literally tore off my left arm and began gnawing on it.

"Ducky, why are you doing this?"

When I tried to run out the front door, he grabbed me and roughly crammed me into the cupboard under the sink. He then continued to gnaw on my severed arm. I lay there, bleeding profusely, trying to make sense of it all. Where had I gone wrong? What could I have done to prevent this?

As I began to feel cold and my vision dimmed, a realization came to me. It was something that I had not dared allow myself to even ponder. I missed Jean.

Ecoli's Meats

ECOLI'S MEAT SHOP was in the east end of the city, surrounded by pawnshops, cheap cafés, and pornographic theaters. Antonio Ecoli spent all of his days with a knife in hand. He hardly noticed anything in the world other than the pattern made by strands of fat in a muscle.

His wife and child lived in the apartment above, and he neither wanted nor received help from them, instead taking on a young assistant for a very low wage, who could be seen in the alley emptying buckets of blood.

Mr. Ecoli's son, the double-nosed dwarf Umberto, was born to a mother whose only ambition in life was to run off to Asia with a handsome young lover. A homely short, thickset woman, her dream would go unfulfilled. She dreamed of flat stomachs and romantic dinners. She had to admit it to herself—Ecoli's ever-present odor of gore was a real turnoff.

She paid little attention to her tiny child and kept him in a dresser drawer until his fifth birthday while she sat listlessly at the window, watching for handsome strangers.

Up until his first day of school, Umberto had never been in the company of anyone but his mother, father, and a midwife who hadn't been able to help herself from commenting, "I don't like his chances." His parents refused to take him out in public, out of shame for his stunted, warped body and two noses. They had only sent him to school because a government bureaucrat threatened a fine of $450, but once the teachers saw his ugliness and two noses, they sent him home immediately so as to not disturb the other pupils.

When Umberto returned home early on his first and only day of school, there was no one home to let him in, and not having a key, he crawled through the cat door. When he tried to climb into the dresser drawer, he found that his stomach had grown too fat to close himself in, and he had to lie in the laundry hamper. Umberto told his parents that the teacher had said he would have to go to a school for children with two noses. They never attempted to locate such a school and were glad they didn't have to take him out in public anymore. Eventually, he would take a place beside his mother at the window. She watched the young men; he, the beautiful women. His mother tried to keep him off the windowsill, but he held on with the iron grip of short, thick dwarf's fingers, and she couldn't pry him off. Not wanting to be seen next to her son, she abandoned the window and instead drew sketches of square-jawed men with Roman noses that she could never get quite right.

So the neighborhood became aware of the dwarf in the window above Ecoli's Meats.

Umberto stared at the women with wide-eyed, innocent fascination. He didn't notice their boyfriends and husbands, who shook their fists at him, shouting threats, and throwing rocks up at the window, although they never broke a single pane. With dumb longing, he hovered above the crowds.

Umberto's favorite was a woman with pitch-black hair, large breasts, and cold, uncompromising eyes. She looked at him just the same way his mother did. She walked past the window each day with her husband to buy coffee. She saw Umberto in the window and hated him. She was beautiful; he was ugly—the enemy. And one day as the sun fell, she beckoned him down with a crooked finger, twirling a perfect satin tress around another. In the light of the street lamps, Umberto saw that she was the most beautiful and enigmatic thing in the world. He couldn't resist taking down a rose from the vase in which his mother kept the flowers that she pretended were from a twenty-five-year-old weight lifter/poet from Prague.

Umberto never expected cruelty even though that's all he'd ever been fed. He assumed that if he just kept living, then something nice would happen. It might be the very next moment. He never could have imagined that a trap had been set for him in the deserted alley where the dark-haired woman waited for him. Or that her husband would cut out his eyes out with a fillet knife. He never truly understood what a cruel world waited for him below the window.

Umberto rolled in the dirty puddles of his own blood and that of other forgotten animals. The couple ran away, not laughing, not smiling, but satisfied in some primal way. They were never caught, and they rarely ever thought about what they'd done. Umberto, blinded as he was, somehow made his way to the cat door and crawled in.

Ecoli's assistant had witnessed this scene from the shadows of the alley, standing motionless and holding a bucket of diseased livers in each hand. When it was all over, he walked slowly to the door and saw the trail of blood leading in, but he didn't hear Umberto's whimpering as he lay in the laundry hamper upstairs. The assistant stood there for a while, wondering what he should do. Ecoli had been waiting impatiently to refill the buckets and went looking for him and found him in a trance, staring at the door. Ecoli berated him, calling him a lazy half-wit. The assistant didn't look up. Then slowly removing his apron, he replied, "I must be a half-wit to work for you. Eight hours a day, up to my elbows in blood."

Teflon

MICHELLE WAS QUITE a catch. Everything about her was perfect—her long blond curls, those perfect ripe breasts, not too big and not too small, just nice handfuls. Beautifully soft and supple skin, green eyes, a cute little nose and well-formed ears. And those buttocks, my word. So firm and smooth, perfect. She had a dancer's rear, and she was, in fact, a dancer. She had the kind of body that only comes with hard work, and I appreciated that. She kept herself very clean, which I also appreciated, as I am a clean freak.

I keep my apartment spotless. Sunday afternoon is the big cleaning day, usually six to seven hours of solid, perspiring work. Of course I'm constantly tidying and keeping an eye out for any offending particles. I pay special attention to the bathroom. The bathroom is, as all people know, a literal incubator for germs and bacteria. The bathroom must be kept clean—the walls, floor, sink, and toilet must be constantly disinfected. For obvious reasons the toilet needs daily attention.

A mutual friend had set Michelle and I up on a blind date, and when I met her at the restaurant, I could barely believe my luck. The dinner went wonderfully, and she talked constantly about her life and the various relationships that her friends were involved in. All the time she was speaking, I was completely fixated on how aesthetically pleasing and well proportioned she was. The fact the she ordered nothing more than a small green salad for dinner was a bonus. There is nothing more unpleasant than watching and hearing a woman devour a bloody steak or a big stinking plate of meat lasagna. The last thing I need is to spend a night with someone going through the gruesome process of digesting a lump of flesh, knowing that at some point they would skulk away to release foul odors and matter.

Anyway, she seemed thoroughly charmed by my wit and sophistication, and that night I brought her to my apartment and, of course, bedded her. We were soon seeing each other regularly. We went to the theater once a week(Friday), for dinner twice per week (Saturday and Tuesday), and jogging every Wednesday. She continued to eat sparingly and always ate clean foods, such as lettuce and apples. It was a great relief to have met a woman that I did not have to admonish over her diet.

One morning it all began to fall apart. Michelle had an early meeting at the office and had gotten ready and left before I woke up. As soon as I stepped into the bathroom that morning, I knew that something was amiss—just the slightest hint of a pong. I approached the toilet warily. At first I didn't notice the cause, but upon closer inspection, I found that the upper ring of the bowl was speckled with brown particles, just below the rim. I quickly flushed, but it was no use; they were stuck. I removed them manually and then disposed of the toilet brush. Suddenly my opinion of and respect for Michelle was shaken.

I sincerely tried to soldier on, as if nothing of importance had occured. We continued our weekly regimen of movie, dinner, and the gym. Sexually, I continued to perform well but with somewhat less enthusiasm—the memory of what I had been subjected to was still vivid. I had seen past her facade, and I did not like it. I would try to see her as the porceline figurine we both wished her to be, but the stain of mortality was already upon her.

I knew that it was only a matter of time before the other shoe dropped, and so I decided to act. The idea came to me as I was making whole wheat crepes in my new German frying pan, apparently the same brand that Elton John's chef uses. Teflon. Why had I never thought of it, Michelle aside, just for my own use. After some effort, I managed to contact the pan company and elicit from them the brand of Teflon used on their pans. At considerable cost, I arranged for a tub of it to be flown overseas from some awful Eastern European country. I believe it was called Romouldia. For some reason the plumber that I hired to coat the toilet bowl with the Teflon didn't seem to understand my request. "Let me explain this one more time. I merely require that you empty my toilet bowl and then coat it with this industrial Teflon, which I have had flown in at considerable cost." Eventually, the poor buffoon relented and applied the coating generously, just as I had requested. Once the job was done and the plumber out of my house, I sat back, sipped a glass of excellent red wine, and breathed a heavy sigh, both physical and spiritual. It looked like everything was going to turn out just fine after all.

Michelle broke up with me that night, by BlackBerry, just as I would have done. It is much more tasteful to break up by BlackBerry—it is, all in all, much cleaner. Her reasoning was sound, the note clear and concise. I realized that she deserved more respect than I had ever afforded her. She believed that I had been the one to smatter the upper toilet rim. Whichever one of us that had committed the crime, it hardly mattered. In any case, it is for the best, and deep down I understood that she would never be the same for me; she was diminished in my eyes just as I was diminished in hers. It was time, for both of us, to begin again with a clean slate. Flush.

The Package

T HE TROUBLE ALL started when John received a package in the mail. It was a box wrapped in white paper and tied with string. No return address. This is what first drew John's concern—that he should receive an unexpected package with no return address. He called his parents, but they hadn't sent it. He called a friend who taught English in Korea, but he knew nothing of it. Eventually, after watching it sit on the dining table for several hours, he put it underneath the kitchen sink.

John's first thought each morning was of the box and what it might contain. At work, he considered the problem of the box, and as soon as he returned home, he would look under the sink. He called everyone that he knew and then everyone that he had ever known. Many of these calls caused both parties a varying degree of embarrassment.

At first, on occasion, John would bring out the package and attempt to begin the process of opening it; but immediately upon laying his fingers on the string, he would recoil in fear. He was not a man used to taking risks. He did not like the unexpected, and he could not imagine anything more unusual than receiving such a package. He came to the conclusion that it must be one of two things: either a bomb or merely a harmless package intended for someone else.

He did not have any enemies—he was certain of that, so if it were a bomb it would have to be the work of some deranged loner, much like the Unabomber whom he had seen on television. It was most likely, he told himself, that he was being paranoid to some extent. He knew that the odds of receiving a mail bomb were exceedingly low, as likely as being hit by a meteor, but it was possible, and one could not discount the notion.

He racked his memory to think of where it might have come from. Was it possible, he wondered, that he'd ordered something in the mail and then forgotten? No, he hadn't ordered anything through the mail—he was certain. Perhaps it was some sort of mix-up. The box may contain an electric toothbrush or some manner of abdominal exerciser.

He decided to ignore the package. He went about his usual business and thought less and less about it. Soon his sleep improved, and he began to look healthier and gained several pounds. Guilt over his temporary paranoia caused him to immerse himself in his work, and soon he received a promotion. He was presented with new business cards that read General Manager above his name. With his increased salary, he bought himself new Italian shoes, a silk shirt, and a tailored suit. The morning before work, he modeled his new clothes in the mirror as he pretended to exchange cards with people of importance. His self-esteem had never been so high.

He had become so comfortable with the presence of the box that he no longer checked on it or thought of opening it. He had learned to coexist with it.

Armed with his newfound success, he was soon dating a lithe young secretary named Mary, whose vivid red lipstick had always garnered his attention. But as their relationship progressed to intercourse, it was stalled by his chronic premature ejaculatory response. He consulted men's magazines to find a cure and discovered in one article that in such cases it was beneficial to distract oneself with nonsexual thoughts and imagery. Thus, during subsequent couplings, he mentally ran through the rosters of various sports teams, but to little effect. Not even the questions it raised

R. T. BARNES

about the boundaries of his sexuality interrupted the rapid resolution of his climax. Clearly, he thought, he must up the ante. He imagined tarantulas crawling on Mary's breasts, and then he saw her as a decomposing corpse, but this strategy only succeeded in creating an ever-growing sense of self-loathing and shame.

Soon he found that he was unable to conjure any thoughts or images at all during sex, and he surrendered to his urges altogether. Night after night he continued, heedlessly following a policy of quantity over quality, all the while seeing the gradual withering of enthusiasm on Mary's part and looking down on an increasingly bored face. And so it was, that one night, just as he felt himself surrendering to his natural tendency, the blank face of his lover was replaced by the image of the mysterious box. To his relief, this did distract him somewhat, and he was able to continue for several minutes longer than usual. Encouraged by this, he tried again as soon as he had recovered and managed to extend himself an additional few minutes.

He wondered how such a simple and obvious solution had eluded him. As it happened, he concluded, the arrival of the package had been a hidden blessing. In fact, it had brought him nothing but good fortune. Each night, his stamina increased, and soon his lover was ecstatically declaring her unbounded love for him. She asked him if he'd begun to take some form of medication. He told her he'd simply begun to exercise a greater control of himself, likely due to his rising self-confidence.

Eventually, Mary began to notice that during their lovemaking John seemed preoccupied, and although his eyes were fixated on her face, his own face was blank, and he seemed to look through her. She wondered if he was imagining that he was making love to another woman.

Riddled with jealousy, she demanded to know what he was thinking. John, still euphoric in his method, told her the story of the box and how it had provided him with the sexual stamina that he'd for so long pined.

She listened without comment although her image of him was badly shaken by what she considered to be highly abnormal behavior.

She turned onto her side, staring into the darkness as John fell asleep. That he was clearly relieved by his confession brought Mary little comfort. Soon John was sleeping heavily, walruslike noises coming from his nose and preventing any possibility of sleep for Mary. As she lay, wide-awake and solitary on her side of the bed, she thought of the box, struggling to understand John's fixation. *It's just a box*, she thought. *What can the harm be in a box?* That it might be a mail bomb was a concept too fantastic for her. Clearly, she thought, it must have been a mix-up at the post office, and there might even be something valuable in it—vague images filled her imagination, of gold and silver, luxurious fur of a rare species; any manner of joyous surprises might have been lying wasted under the kitchen sink.

*

After the explosion, John impressed his coworkers with an impeccable professionalism. He didn't feel the need to burden his peers with his grief, and if anything, he was more productive than ever. It was an unspoken rule at the office that the box incident should never be discussed in John's presence, and a short time later, when he was promoted to regional manager, the matter was largely forgotten.

The Most Beautiful Music in the World

DAVID DID NOT own a coffeemaker. His mother had given him a new one the previous Christmas, and David had been much impressed by its timer feature, which enabled him to set it the night before and wake up to a freshly brewed pot of coffee, which he loved. David couldn't start his day without a fresh cup of coffee—he didn't feel awake until he'd had one. Sadly, one morning he found that his kitchen was engulfed in flames. He put out the blaze with a small household fire extinguisher that his cousin, a firefighter, had given him as a birthday present. After a short investigation by the insurance company, the coffeemaker was determined as the cause, due to a design flaw in the wiring. David did not make coffee at home after that; it was simply too dangerous. From then on David went to the Shop Mart convenience store for his cup of morning coffee.

One morning as David approached the Shop Mart, he anxiously regarded a man who wore a tattered USA jacket and stained cargo pants standing by the entrance. The man was blowing into a didgeridoo. David called him the Droning Man, due to the drone of the instrument. The Droning Man was standing by the entrance through which David needed to pass. The drone of the didgeridoo filled David's head, as it did each morning and every other time that he went into the Shop Mart. The Droning Man was always there.

David steeled himself for the first daily coin toss,that moment when he would cross the threshold, enter into the store, with his eyes locked firmly ahead and away from the Droning Man. When he would either pass unmolested or the dreadful other thing would happen. He might hear the only words that the Droning Man spoke. The Droning Man spoke with utter despair. He would say, his voice thin and reedy, "I have an infected spleen." It was a plea. It demanded action. David knew that a decent person should act in this case. He knew that there was no choice for a man such as himself. He did not know how a man's spleen could become infected, or the consequences of such a malady; but he knew that he must act, over and over again, if he were asked. If he were not asked, then it was not his fault, and he bore no responsibility. Upon entering, David was not asked, but it did nothing to quell his anxiety; he still had to exit the store. Perhaps he'll leave while I'm in here, David thought as he prepared his coffee, although he knew this was a vain hope. Once it might have been so, but those days had passed; the Droning Man's stamina was inconceivable, and he would remain right where he was, day and night.

As David waited in line to pay for his coffee, he reflected on his disdain for the didgeridoo. It did not, he thought, deserve to be called an instrument. To play the didgeridoo was to do nothing more than blow into a piece of wood. He had heard some nonsense about circular breathing patterns and the like but remained unimpressed. How hard is breathing, circular or not? David imagined a past Droning Man, futilely attempting to learn the keyboards, then guitar, then bongo, and failing even at that, finally hitting rock bottom—didgeridoo. Anyone can blow into a piece of wood, David assured himself as he paid the teller.

David approached the door, eyes fixed on the floor ahead, head cocked slightly to the opposite direction of the Droning Man, but not enough to appear rude, just enough to make him appear preoccupied by something other than the sound of didgeridoo. He opened the door and quickened his pace.

"I have an infected spleen . . ." The instrument paused only for a moment, just long enough for the statement—the demand. David

R. T. BARNES

stopped in midstride, fixed the Droning Man with a forced smile, and searched his pockets for change. He threw fifty-five cents into the cap at the man's feet. The Droning Man nodded appreciatively and then focused on his playing with a greater enthusiasm. David could still hear the *bwaaa bwaaa bwaaa* of the didgeridoo as he drove out of the lot.

It all seemed very unfair to David. He asked himself, "Can I afford to give change to panhandlers? Yes. Do I want to give change to panhandlers? Not really." David considered himself to be a modestly generous man; he always put change into the little tin cups that shopkeepers kept by the till, the ones with pictures of unfortunate children with a variety of issues, always serious—the ones with a genuine right to beg from him. So David did not consider himself an unkind man. It was the constancy of the Droning Man and the passive-aggressive nature of his assault on David's conscience that bothered him. David didn't want to be a bad person, and so he had to prove himself, over and over again, to the Droning Man.

That evening, on his way home from work, David decided that he wanted bacon and sour cream potato chips to snack on after dinner while he watched TV. He did not go to the Shop Mart. He drove ten blocks past the Shop Mart to the Happy Face Mart. David didn't like to go out of his way; he much preferred to go to his regular mart, as it was only one block from his apartment and required less driving. David didn't like to drive. David was a nervous driver, always expecting catastrophe. He was fully confident in his own driving skill. It was the others that he feared. He noted disapprovingly all of his fellow drivers' dangerous foibles. Speeding, running yellow and red lights, failure to signal—David knew well the dangers of the road. Yet it was worth the anxiety of extra driving if it meant he could escape the judgment of the Droning Man.

As David pulled into the parking lot of the Happy Face Mart, he saw the Droning Man standing by the entrance, looking directly at him.

David turned his head quickly away, as if he had not noticed the Droning Man, and drove straight through the lot and back onto the street. He drove back toward the Shop Mart, upset that he had exposed himself to additional driving risk for no reason. He consoled himself that he would now surely be able to buy potato chips without discomfort, he could walk right through the entrance with a clear conscience. Perhaps the Droning Man had decided to switch locations? David felt a triumphant joy at the thought.

David was shocked and dismayed to discover the Droning Man was standing in front of the Shop Mart as well. David did not stop; he drove directly home, his hands shaking. There must be two Droning Men, twins in fact, he concluded. And not only were they identical twins, but they both wore the same USA jackets and cargo pants. Suddenly things had become more complicated. As David sat down at his kitchen table for dinner that night, a terrible thought came to him—perhaps the Droning Man had become a franchise, that the city was slowly filling with more and more Droning Men by the day? Soon there might be no convenience store without the constant rumble of *bwaaa bwaaa bwaaa*. But no, the two men had been *identical*; it was clearly some sort of family affair.

David lay sleepless for several hours that night, angry that he had been prevented from satisfying his hunger for potato chips, which, for being a taxpayer he deserved, and swearing to himself that he would not allow himself to be denied his morning coffee and that most importantly, he would not give change to the Droning Man, no matter how pathetic his plea.

In the morning, David gave change to the Droning Man both going in and leaving the Shop Mart. He forgave himself while driving to work, reasoning that his powers were weakened by his poor night's sleep; it angered him that the Droning Man could weaken his powers at will.

R. T. BARNES

When he arrived at work, the Droning Man was there at the front entrance, playing didgeridoo. David panicked and fled back home but as he neared the entrance to his apartment building, he heard the slow *bwaaa bwaaa bwaaa* of the hated didgeridoo. David peeked from behind a bush and saw, as he knew he would, the Droning Man. The playing stopped for a moment, and the words "I have a diseased spleen" floated to him on the wind, like a plea. David peeked again, and the Droning Man was looking in his direction. David fled to his mother's house and finally found a safe haven, a place without a Droning Man at the door. He couldn't go back to his apartment, and so this would be his home now. He hurriedly let himself in. His mother was sitting on the couch with a cup of tea and several gingersnaps. "Hello, son," she said merrily as he dropped to the couch next to her. "I have wonderful news."

David was exhausted from the stress of the previous few days and told her that he needed a rest and he was going to his old bedroom and take a short nap, and then they could have a good chat, and after that she could make them dinner. As he started down the hall, he noticed a low droning sound, which grew louder as he neared the closed door of his childhood bedroom. He stood in front of the door, afraid to open it. He asked his mother why there was droning coming from his room and what it was. She replied, "Something wonderful! Something just wonderful!"

David opened the door slowly, with his eyes closed, as his head filled with the deep droning. He swayed on his feet, falling into a deep hypnotic state, the sound rising, incredibly loud, as if there were a thousand didgeridoos all around him. David could no longer keep his balance and opened his eyes, desperately grasping for the doorframe, and then steadied himself. The Droning Man was sitting on David's bed, playing didgeridoo, not seeming to notice David; he was enraptured by his own playing. The USA jacket and cargo pants were on the floor—the

Droning Man was wearing David's old Looney Tunes pajamas, which fit quite well, and David was surprised that he had never noticed how small the Droning Man was. The droning became louder still, and the room began to spin; and David lost his grip and fell clumsily to the floor, his limbs splayed about. His mother stood over him laughing and clapping her hands. "Listen. Listen! Isn't it wonderful!" she shouted.

David listened. He closed his eyes. He was in a universe of droning, and then he noticed a melody. It was a song. With his eyes closed he saw a billion stars, and then was floating among them. Then there were drums . . . and then guitars . . . and then vocals, and then he finally understood what he was hearing. The song was perfect, the droning gone. David knew that he would never again hear a more beautiful rendition of "Stairway to Heaven," or any other song, not ever, not if he lived for a thousand years. He searched his pockets for change.

R. T. BARNES

Made in the USA
Charleston, SC
11 May 2011